A NEW DEATH

Josh Vasquez

This book is a work of fiction. Names, characters, places and incidents are the product of the author's imagination or are used fictitiously. Any resemblance to actual events, locales, or persons, living or dead (or undead), is coincidental.

ISBN-13: 978-1495239472
ISBN-10: 1495239470

Copyright © 2013 by Joshua Vasquez

Second Edition Paperback September 2014

All rights reserved.

Cover design and additional artwork by Xavier Martinez

To my Laura,
To whom this book would not be possible.

"There's too many people in this world. We need a new plague."

Dwight Schrute

Prologue

The marsh had been extremely pungent this afternoon. All day it had stunk, but this afternoon it seemed to be so much stronger. Brad Wilcox noticed the smell continued to grow as time slowly ticked away. His partner, JW, didn't seem fazed by it one bit. The old man was much accustomed to the tidal scent of the low country. The man grew old on this smell.

Brad, on the other hand, was relatively new to it. And he hated it. Having moved from up north near Chicago, he had yet to be indoctrinated in the coastal South's muggy summer evenings and marsh-stink. He was use to city smells like traffic exhaust and refineries. How he ended up down here in Savannah was a story in itself.

His ex-wife was born and raised here, so of course once they got married, they had to move back here. She just had to be near her family. Brad left his good-paying office job in the city to come down and work for his father-in-law's landscaping company. Which was fine, he had no problem working for the man, or hard labor, except for the fact that once they got divorced, he lost his job too. She cheats on him, so he loses his job. Makes perfect sense, doesn't it?

And that's pretty much how he ended up here on this god-forsaken boat in the middle of the stinking marsh. More or less. When the economy tanked, he didn't have many choices on the job front. A friend found him this job and when you're broke, you'll take anything.

"Does it always smell this bad?" he asked.

"What smell?" huffed the old man.

Brad heard him swear under his breath. He decided to ignore it, as the two men had already had their post-civil war conversations. It's amazing how after over a hundred and fifty years, the resentment for each other still lingered between the north and south. Brad didn't even consider himself a Yankee. He was originally from Virginia, which if you knew your history, was a part of the Confederacy. But if you come up from up north, and you have an inkling of an opinion, you just became a "damn Yankee." Brad could care less what the old redneck had to say.

Their small fishing boat puttered along the coastal waterway. He didn't have all the names down yet, but if he remembered right, this was Turner's Creek. It had been a pretty unsuccessful day. All they were returning to dock with was empty nets and sour attitudes. Brad saw the dock off in the distance. Too far it seemed. This day seemed to have lasted forever. In the hot Georgia heat, five minutes seemed like forever, much less ten hours. The only thing that mattered to Brad right now was the frosty six pack of cold beer at the house.

Brad walked to the front of the boat to the anchor hoist. It was rusty and slow, but still better than dragging the chain up by hand. He had the anchor on the deck by the time they pulled up to the dock. The two dock hands, Julio and Alberto, were there waiting on them, ready to secure the boat and the equipment.

They were good guys, illegal, but good guys nonetheless. Brad didn't know what loop holes they jumped through to get their jobs, but that's the thing with illegal immigrants; they're cheap labor. And the guys didn't care. Most of what they made, they sent back to their families in Mexico and what they didn't, they spent on tequila and beer. Brad spent many a night getting shit-faced with the two amigos.

As Brad began to put things away, the two dock hands and JW began to secure the boat to the floating dock. He put the few fishing poles they had back onto the racks, but as he did, he noticed something floating nearby the shore. At first, he didn't recognize what the shape was, but very quickly his mind figured out the familiar object. It was a human body.

"There's a body in the river!" he yelled, jumping into the shallow, brackish water.

The three others took notice of the alarm in Brad's voice and ran along the shore to where Brad was standing. He reached the body, which he now knew to be a young, Asian woman's. He grabbed her by the shoulders, yanking her down-turned face out of the water.

"Miss! You alright?!"

Her body was limp. Cold. Lifeless.

"Lady?" This time more concern filled his voice.

Nothing. JW kneeled down at the shore. His face had softened. It was no longer the stern, grumpy face that he sported at all times. This face was much gentler. More concerned.

"Brad..." he said.

"LADY!" Brad screamed, giving the woman's body a firm shake.

"Brad," JW tried again.

"We gotta do something. CPR or something!" Brad shouted.

JW just shook his head.

"Brad," he started. "She's gone..."

Brad couldn't believe him. He kept looking at the girl's pale white face, thinking to himself that she couldn't be dead. This can't be real. This isn't the way his day was supposed to end. Hell, this wasn't the way her life was supposed to end.

Not like this. Not like this, he thought to himself.

He closed his eyes tight, trying to see if he could wake up from this nightmare. He tried to put himself somewhere else, somewhere happier. At home, with his beer. But as he was trying to focus his mind elsewhere, he felt movement in his arms. His eyes shot back open to see the girl beginning to stir back to life.

"She's alive!" he yelled.

The others lifted up their heads to see. Julio and Alberto began to smile and light up, but JW look worried. Something was not right in his mind.

Something was not right.

She moaned.

"She's alive! She's alive!" Brad yelped.

She moaned again, this time louder and longer. She seemed in pain or agony. Her hands slowly but stiffly grabbed onto Brad's arms. Her body seemed rigid and tense.

"Miss? You all right? What happened?" Brad asked rapid fire.

She froze. Her head slowly tilted to the left, looking Brad directly in the face. When she moved her head, she revealed a fatal looking wound in her neck. It was a dark purple and reeked of infection.

"Ma'am? You okay?"

Brad began to grow uneasy. That wound looked like it should have killed her. Actually, there should be no reason to why she was moving right now. It was then that the look of concern on JW's face made sense. This woman should have been dead.

Her eyes shot open. They were pitch black; her pupils non-existent. Brad tried to set her back down, but her grasp tightened around his arms as she began to pull him in closer. He struggled to push her off of him and began to panic.

"Lady, let go!" he yelled.

There's no way she should be this strong, she's so tiny, his mind raced.

But despite her small frame, the woman pulled him closer, her jaw moving up and down. JW jumped into the water and began to try and pry the young woman off of Brad. Both men struggled to fight off the tiny woman's unwelcome advances. JW slipped on the river bottom, falling backwards, and giving the girl enough momentum to lunge forwards.

She sank her teeth into Brad's neck.

He screamed as the others watched on in horror. She continued to bite down on his neck. Her teeth taking out huge chunks of meat. Brad no longer fought back. He felt his body slip into shock. The pain both excruciating and numbing at the same time. His eyes began to roll back into his head, his body convulsing. JW rushed back to his feet, while Julio and Alberto ran away screaming. He grabbed the girl, this time successfully pulling her away from Brad. But as he pulled her off, she turned, using the motion and sunk her teeth into JW's face. Brad sunk into the water, breathing his last remaining breaths. Blood spurted from his exposed jugular, turning the surrounding water a brownish-red.

JW was now screaming as the girl began to eat his face. He could barely hold her at bay. The blood poured down his face, his eyes burning. He used what last bit of energy he had to give one final push, knocking the deranged woman off of him and over to the side. He could barely see, his own blood obscuring his vision. His face seemed numb around the bite marks.

He scrambled back a few feet on his backside. Wiping what blood he could away from his eyes, he noticed that there were now two shadows standing over him.

The girl.

And Brad.

Brad's neck was no longer bleeding, but the same dark, purple as the girl's open wound. His eyes were also now black, and he moaned in agony, just as the girl had earlier.

"Brad?" JW asked, wondering if his partner could still understand him.

Brad, or whatever you call the shell of him, looked at JW with a dead stare. His mouth began to move up and down, teeth clattering. The two shambled towards JW and began to finish what the girl had started.

JW screamed, but quickly went silent as Brad ripped into his abdomen, spilling the old man's intestines into the mud. The two dead kneeled down and began to eat the man while he was still alive.

Chapter One

Jeremy Riggins sat in the break room, procrastinating about going back to work. Brian, his douche of a manager, told him before his ten minute break that when he was done, Jeremy was on shopping cart duty. Jeremy hated shopping cart duty. What made it worse was that Jeremy was a cashier, not one of the courtesy clerks. They were short a few people that day, so Brian told Jeremy to close his register, and take care of the carts.

Now, the carts weren't below Jeremy; he had no problem doing what needed to be done. He was a team player. He just didn't like Brian. Brian was one of those guys who, once they got a little authority, liked to flaunt it and abuse it. Everybody was now his peon. He must have had a rough life in high school and now it was his turn to be on top of the food chain.

Jeremy downed the last sip of his energy drink and tossed the can into the recycling. He slowly made his way back downstairs. He was in no hurry. It was way too hot outside. Middle of November and still ninety degrees out. He was already wearing his work polo and khakis. Add the reflective vest he had to wear while in the parking lot and you had one extremely sweaty Jeremy.

As he passed by the registers towards the time clock, Ashley smiled at him, and mouthed the word, 'sorry.' He nodded. She felt bad for him.

Great, he thought. *The pity card isn't exactly the way I wanted to work things.*

The two of them had just started "talking". Jeremy had yet to work up the nerve to ask her to go see a movie or something. Timing just hadn't been right. But now that he was going to be all hot and sweaty bagging her groceries, now seemed like the opportune time.

Jeremy clocked back in, grabbed the safety vest off the rack, and then began to make his way outside. He soaked in the store's air conditioning, mentally preparing himself for the sauna outside. Savannah's heat wasn't just hot, it was humid too. Within a minute, he'd be drenched.

"Jeremy!"

He turned to see Brian behind him. His large, obtuse belly hung over his belt, and his hands were sitting on his hips. The man was tall, which probably led to more awkwardness and ridicule in his teen years.

"Hurry up with the carts. We need you back in here bagging too."

"I can't be in two places at once, Brian," Jeremy said. "Maybe you should bag while I'm out there frying in the sun."

Jeremy noticed Ashley giggle, but Brian turned bright red. This wasn't the first time that Jeremy shot back at him, but it always produced the same results.

"Just hurry back in here!"

He pointed towards the doors. Jeremy started to say something else, but decided against it.

What was the point?

***

"I hate my job."

Jeremy whined to himself as he pushed the train of shopping carts back towards the building. It was hot. Just like he knew it was going to be. His clothes were drenched in sweat. The sweat dripped off his forehead like a heavy summer rain. Except that, this summer, there was no rain. Just heat. And sun.

He pushed the carts back into their appropriate place within the building and turned back to the parking lot to continue his torture of collecting them all.

"Sweet Jesus, it's way too hot for this," he mumbled to himself.

Jeremy watched as a woman on the opposite side of the parking lot pushed her cart onto a curb, got in her car, and drove off. The very action annoyed him down to his core. Her car was two parking spots away from a cart corral. Two.

"Why can't you people put the carts back into the corrals? It's not that hard of a concept! You take a cart, you put it back! It's not rocket science!" He asked out loud as an elderly woman passed by.

She didn't seem to be too amused by Jeremy's tone, because she huffed and scurried herself into the store. He let out a sigh and walked towards the rogue buggy. She was probably going to go complain to the manager. Who just so happened to be Brian. He thought about the lecture he was going to receive once he was done with the carts.

And that's when he heard the screaming. Screams came from inside the building. Blood-curdling screams. The kind you don't run to and investigate. Jeremy left the buggies in the middle of the road and sprinted for the store. He ran in past the door and stopped dead in front of the registers. It was there he saw something he thought he would never see.

A human eating another human.

There really is no way to prepare yourself for that kind of thing. A small, Asian woman was hunched over the register, clawing and biting the face of one of the cashiers. There was blood everywhere. So much bright-red, fresh blood. His hand went to his mouth, as if to hold back the impending vomit, but nothing came. The scene had shocked him so badly that it took him a moment to realize who was being attacked.

It was Ashley.

Jeremy's mouthed opened to scream, "No!", but no sound came out. He was frozen in place as the woman began to maul the girl he'd been dying to take out to a movie. The store was in full panic now. Customers were running, knocking things over, and bumping into each other. Some even tried to make off with their groceries. Brian ran up to the woman attacking Ashley. On top of being a huge douche, Brian was also not very bright. He was holding a mop.
Yeah, good choice Brian, Jeremy thought.
He swung. Missed. Swung again, missed, and lost his balance. He tumbled forwards, arms flailing, into the woman. She lurched forward and began ripping and tearing into her new snack. It all was happening so fast it almost looked choreographed. Things this bad couldn't run so smoothly. Jeremy barely had any time to react. He quickly snapped out of it and grabbed the mop from the floor.

"Ma'am!" he yelled. "I'm going to need you to stop eating Brian!"

Perhaps yelling at the person who just started eating people's faces off was not such a good idea. She lost interest in eating Brian and was now completely focused on Jeremy. She moaned and began to shamble over towards him. He swung the mop back and forth, trying to keep a good safe distance between the two of them.

"Lady! Back off!" he shouted.

She didn't listen. She didn't even seem to comprehend. She just continued to claw at him; her jaw clamping up and down. Jeremy realized there was no reasoning with her. She was insane. The car was running, but there was nobody behind the wheel-kinda thing. He swung the mop again, but this time she caught the mop head, breaking it off from the handle.

"Great, now all I have is this pointy stick..." he muttered to himself.

Instinct kicked in and he jabbed her in the right arm. The splintered wood sank into her flesh like a hot knife into a tub of butter. He expected screaming and pain, but it didn't faze her one bit. No grimace, no shrieks. She just continued to try and eat Jeremy. He was not going to let her do that.

A rage sunk over Jeremy, a kind of anger he never felt before. Something primal, something buried deep within him. He yanked back on his makeshift spear, pulling free from her arm. The jolt sent her back a few steps. She regained her footing and came at him again. He hit her again, this time square in the right lung. Nothing. Again no screaming or any signs of pain.

What in the world is going on?

He yanked back on the mop again, freeing the handle. She lost her balance again, but quickly was right back on top of Jeremy. This could not be happening.

She should be dead right now...

The anger rose up in him. He set his feet, let out a yell, and lurched forward, sinking the stick directly into the girl's eye socket. It sunk in deep and she fell to her knees, then to the floor. She was dead. For good this time.

Sweet Jesus, what did I just do? He thought to himself. *I had to. I had no choice. It was self-defense. I just had to. She wouldn't stop...*

As Jeremy reasoned with himself, trying to find some reason to make what just happened okay, or believable for that matter. The store was empty now. All the customers and the rest of the staff were long gone. It was now just Jeremy and three dead bodies. One of which, was because of his doing.

"Uhh..."

A moan came from Ashley's collapsed body. Jeremy

ran over to her and knelt down next to her. He pulled her up into his arms. She was still alive. Her breath was shallow, her breathing affected by the loose, mangled skin covering her face. She looked completely unrecognizable to him. The only thing that Jeremy could connect with her former self was her bright, blue eyes, which seemed much more vibrant compared to the ground hamburger look of her face.

"Ashley," was all he could muster up.

He sat there and watched as she died in his arms. Her body tensed and then relaxed as she breathed her last strained breath. She was dead. Jeremy sat there for a moment, soaking in everything that was happening. He was having a hard time believing it. He so desperately wanted to be dreaming, but he knew that just was not the case. He laid Ashley back down on the floor gently.

What the hell is going on? I just killed a woman and Ashley just died in my arms. What the hell? And Brian's dead too, but who the fuck cares about Brian?

As he hung his head low, eyes shut tight; he tried to figure out what to do. Mid-thought, he heard movement. The store was still empty. The movement came from in front of him. The girl that just died in his arms, the girl who he felt the life go out of her, was now getting back onto to her knees and attempting to stand back up. This was not good. There was no thinking, "Oh, good! She's alive!" No, this felt all wrong. This was not a happy ending.

Jeremy watched on in horror as she began to do the same chomping movement that the other girl had been doing. He tried to slowly back away towards the door, not trying to draw any attention to himself. She didn't seem to notice him. Brian was also making his way to his feet again. The two of them just stood there, in what seemed like a daze. They were aware of each other. Brian tilted his head back and let out a bellowing moan.

It was horrible. Long and drawn out, it was filled with anguish. It seemed to last forever. Jeremy was mere feet from the door, his steps quiet and calculated. There was no need to bring attention to himself. The two newly reanimated corpses began to shuffle around, noses up in the air, sniffing for something. It seemed that Ashley was having trouble, seeing that she had lost her nose. But it quickly dawned on Jeremy what they were sniffing for. They were looking for food. They were looking for him.

As soon as his foot hit outside the doors, he turned and bolted for the back of the building. He had chained his bike up there before his shift. Out of the corner of his eye, he could see that the parking lot was a mess due to all the panic. There were cars smoking from collisions, a few people yelling, but most had just fled the scene. Which was exactly the same thing Jeremy was planning on doing. He had no intentions of sticking around here to see what happened.

His bike was still there, chained to a fire hydrant sticking out from the building. He heard moans in the distance. They were outside the store. He quickly unlocked the chain and jumped on his bike, heading back out towards the front and to the road. He saw both Ashley and Brian on his way out. They were both now attacking the two guys who were arguing over what now seems like a very minor car accident. Jeremy just pressed on.

Peddle like hell, he thought.

He had to get home. And he had to get there quick. Everything was going to hell around him. He had to make sure his mom was okay.

Chapter Two

It seemed as if the whole island was falling apart. Wilmington Island was one of the few coastal islands near Savannah, one that was mostly golf course and suburban sprawl. For a middle to upper class dwelling place, it seemed as if things had shifted upside down, and the apocalypse was upon us. Seeing the dead rise will have that effect on you.

Jeremy never slowed down, pedaling feverishly towards home. As the world crumbled around him, his thoughts were on his mother.

God, I hope she's okay, he thought.

It seemed more like a prayer though. Jeremy was not very religious. He did his time in vacation bible school at the local First Baptist church as a kid, but that was about the extent of his religious background. That was about as much as Jeremy's mother could force on him. Faith was more her thing than it was Jeremy's.

His thoughts went back to his mother, causing his brain to send messages to his legs that they needed to peddle faster. He noticed that there were more people than just Ashley and Brian who were back from the dead.

What did the movies call them? Zombies? The living dead? He thought. *Whatever you call them, there are definitely more of them now.*

It seemed that the woman who initially attacked Ashley was not the only one. There were more. A lot more. As Jeremy raced down the road to his house, he saw probably at least twenty of those things. Nobody he knew, just random people. Some were giving chase to living people, others were being disposed of. Jeremy's mouthed dropped as one woman ran out of her house holding a shotgun, blew the head off one of the zombies, and rushed her kids back inside.

Pulling into the driveway of his house, Jeremy dumped his bike near the side door and ran into the house.

"Mom! Mom, are you home?"

The blinds were still closed, the house dark. It seemed that she was not home from work yet. He fumbled with his phone from his pocket. It was only a quarter to five. She would be home soon. He searched the house just in case one of those things got in somehow. The layout of their house was simple. Two bedrooms on one side of the house, a bathroom in the middle, a living room and a kitchen/dining area taking up the right side of the house. Jeremy checked both his and his mother's bedrooms first. After seeing that they were empty, he checked the bathroom, and then retreated to the living room. He collapsed on the couch and flipped on the TV. The news reports were all over the place.

The news seemed just as confused as Jeremy was about what was going on. The reports were coming from all over the low country. The local news struggled to handle the onslaught of oncoming reports of the dead coming back to life and eating the living. It wasn't until he turned on the major news stations that Jeremy began to worry.

This was not just confined to the islands or Savannah for that matter. This was happening all over the continental United States. Some stations were claiming that the attacks were due to an outbreak in the "bath salts" usage among the homeless. Others were saying it was some sort of airborne biological terrorist attack. The usual names were being thrown around: North Korea, Iran, and even mother Russia herself.

And then you had the loony's, who were fully convinced that this was full on biblical Armageddon. The guy with the big ears was pleading with his viewers to send in money as a faith offering and they would be spared from God's impending wrath. Jeremy didn't know much about the bible, but he knew that wasn't right. No one seemed to know what was exactly going on. Only theories and opinions.

The sound of a car door shutting caused him to jump up to his feet.

She's home!

Relived, he ran to the side door to greet her. She was walking up to the house, a look of intense alarm on her face. His mother had aged well over the years. Her hair was still a bright red, and her skin was remarkably blemish free, except for the few freckles around her cheeks. The only thing that revealed her age was the few strands of gray hair over her ears, probably mostly brought on by Jeremy and his testosterone fueled antics. He would"t claim full responsibility though, he was sure his father and the divorce brought on some as well.

"Jeremy," she started. "You're okay! I was so worried! It seems that everyone is going crazy! I saw this man attack another man. He beat him to the ground and then began to bite him! Can you bel-"

Her words were cut short. Jeremy watched on in shock from the doorway, as a man came shambling out of nowhere, and tackled his mother to the ground. His clothes were tattered and there were stains of blood still fresh around his lips. He put his full weight on her, and began to claw with jagged, broken finger-nails into her skin. His mother held him at bay until, finally, he overpowered her and sunk his teeth into her neck.

"No!" Jeremy screamed.

He flung open the screen door and ran to the rescue of his mother. He ran straight into the ghoul, knocking it off, but he noticed the dark, red blood gushing from his mother's neck. The zombie began to crawl back to the woman it attacked. It was not deterred by Jeremy's tackle. It only wanted to feed.

A flat-head shovel leaning against the fence caught Jeremy's eye. The zombie reached out with its dead hand towards Jeremy's mother. He quickly grabbed the shovel and brought it down hard on the zombie's arm. It moaned in frustration. Jeremy winced as he thrusted the shovel down, over and over again into the dead flesh.

Yes, it was dead flesh, he decided.

It finally broke through bone and tendon, severing the lower arm completely. It moaned again, this time deeper and hoarser. Jeremy now had its full attention.

Jeremy started to turn his attention back to his mother, but another zombie stumbled up the driveway and was making its way towards her. Another was coming across the front yard.

Shit.

He quickly stooped next to his mother and picked her petite frame up into his arms. As he lifted her up, he got a better look at the wound on her neck. It was dark purple and already looked infected. Blood steadily trickled down her neck onto her white blouse.

"Sweet Jesus," he muttered.

She was passed out from the shock. Her body was completely dead weight. Jeremy did his best to carry her back towards the house. He was struggling with getting the door open, when a dead hand took hold of his mother's foot. The two dead had finally caught up to him.

They both lurched at her feet, and with some unhuman strength, pulled her away from him. He watched as his mother was quickly torn limb from limb and devoured. Skin and flesh was torn from the bone. Her arms were pulled out from the sockets; a sickening pop announced the arrival of fresh blood pouring from her arteries. Even the zombie with the severed arm had made its way into the bloodbath.

Tears uncontrollably streamed down his face, as

Jeremy fell back into the house. He locked the deadbolt, and grabbing one of the dining table's chairs, jammed it under the door handle. What should have been a fairly simple task, his mind struggled to focus and he began to feel himself shut down. He felt numb. He fell to his knees in the living room and began to sob.

"No, no, no," he mumbled over and over again.

The dead outside began beating on the door, trying to get in to the food inside. They did not retain the know-how of opening doors. A minor positive amongst the sea of negative. Jeremy began to feel anger wash over him. The same rage he felt in the store, except this time much stronger. He jumped up to his feet and made a beeline for the backyard. He ran outside to the shed, throwing lawn tools aside once he got there, searching for the machete his father left behind after he moved out. Rust had already begun its assault on the large blade.

It'll do, the voice inside his head screamed.

His heart throbbed within his chest and the rage surged throughout his body. Slowly walking up to the gate that led back out front, he paused and remembered his mother. He remembered how she never gave up on him, despite his always rebelling against her. How she was always there for him after his father left. How she prayed for him constantly, despite his wanting nothing to do with her religion. Taking a deep breath and letting the rage burn deep into his lungs, Jeremy flung open the gate, and charged out into the driveway.

The zombies had left the door and returned to his mother's remains. All three looked up in unison. Slowly they stood up and began to walk towards their new meal. This angered Jeremy even more. They were not even satisfied with his mother. Every muscle in Jeremy's body grew tight.

He ran full speed to the nearest corpse and brought

the rusty blade down on its shoulder, cleanly separating the arm from the rest of the body. It moaned, the other two moaning in response. He brought the blade back up and sunk it into the monster's neck. Again. Again. The fourth time sent the head spinning in the air. The body fell limp. It was dead. This time for good.

The other two were not bothered by the fact that their comrade had been killed.

Re-killed? Jeremy quickly thought.

They shambled towards him, arms stretched out, reaching for his warm flesh. Jeremy took another deep breath and let anger replenish his lungs. He sprung forward and quickly disposed of the two remaining dead. Learning from the first one, he did not waste time hacking off limbs. He aimed his blade straight for the neck. Soon their heads joined their friend's on the ground. Their teeth still jawed up and down, until Jeremy took the shovel, and caved in each skull. They would not be getting back up.

It appears from now on, you'll have to kill people twice.

Jeremy felt the rage dissipate; he quickly became exhausted. He went back into the house and locked the door behind him. Heading straight for the bathroom, Jeremy tried to focus. Everything seemed cloudy. He was in a daze. Once in the bathroom, he stood in front of the mirror, steadying himself against the counter. Blood covered him. Not the clean, bright red blood you see in movies. It was coagulated, congealed. Dirty. He stripped off his clothes and stepped into the shower.

Mom, he thought. *She's gone. There was nothing I could do. Was there? No. There wasn't. It was already too late by the time I got to her.*

He continued to replay the scene over and over in his head. The hot water beat against his bare chest, as he tried to figure out some way he could have saved her. There wasn't one. There was simply nothing he could have done different. And he knew that.

When he finished, he went to his room, and stood next to his dresser.

What do you wear for the apocalypse?

Jeremy stared at the drawers, waiting for something to come to him.

Better just keep it simple.

He reached in and pulled out a pair of jeans. They were a light blue, worn around the knees, and sat snug right under his waist. Unlike many of his peers, Jeremy thought that pants should sit at, or just below the waist, not right above your knees. It was hot outside, but the idea of a little extra protection comforted Jeremy. His backpack caught his eye, and he walked over to it, dumping its contents onto the floor.

His first year of college was not really going according to plan. He had decided to stay in town and attend a local school. The main problem was that he worked more than he attended classes. He had scholarships, but he choose not to use them to their full extent. He would never admit it to her, but his mother was the reason he stayed. He did not want to leave her behind.

And now for what? He thought. *She's gone now.*

He quickly put on a plain, black t-shirt, and then began to stuff a second pair of clothes in his bag. A lighter, a pocket knife his father gave him years ago, and his grey Muse hoodie, all made their way into the bag as well. Looking around the room, anything else seemed pointless.

His eyes fell on the small box under his bed. Not really noticeable, but Jeremy knew exactly what it was. It was a surprise his mother never looked in the box or asked about it. Jeremy was convinced that she knew. There was no way she could have been that naive.

He knelt down and retrieved the box. Opening it revealed what was left of some pretty good weed.

Jeremy bought it from a guy a week ago and was slowly burning his way through it. He didn't consider himself a "pothead" or a "stoner"; he didn't bake all the time. It was just something to take the edge off. And now seemed like a really good time to take the edge off. Staring at it, he contemplated smoking a bowl or maybe six.

Just fuck yourself up. Yeah and just ride this shit out...

He shook his head.

And then get torn to pieces by those freaks outside. Get yourself together man; this ain't no time to bake!

He dropped the box on his bed and made his way into the living room. Pausing on his way at his mother's door, he looked in. Everything neatly in its place, still waiting for her to come home. Her bible still sat on her bedside table. Jeremy walked up to it and looked down at the book. The leather cover was cracked and the pages were worn from use. Every morning she got up and read this thing.

And what good did it do her?

It was something she treasured deeply though, perhaps only second to Jeremy himself. He grabbed it and stuffed it into his bag. A picture of the two of them sat next the book. He grabbed that too.

Back in the living room, he gave the room one last look over. He was really stalling for what he was about to do next. Even before the dead started attacking the living, it was one of the last things he wanted to do. He reached for the phone.

"Why am I even bothering?" He asked out loud.

He first dialed his father's cell number. Straight to voicemail. He then redialed his home phone. Answering machine.

"Typical Dad," he sighed.

Regardless of how he felt about his father, the man was now the only family nearby. He would have to go

find him and see if he was okay. Or still alive for that matter.
Fantastic...

Chapter Three

Jeremy took a deep breath before unlocking the door. Stepping outside, he anticipated the worst, but was only greeted by the same grisly scene from earlier. There were no more dead wandering around, just the ones who Jeremy beheaded earlier. He picked up the rusty, bloody machete, and slid it into a strap on his backpack. His bike still lay on its side where he dumped it. He could take his mother's car, but that would require him to find her keys. Avoiding eye contact with his mother's remains, he picked up his bike, and began to ride away from his house.

He thought the island was a mess before. It seemed that this was not going to be a contained incident that some of the media was hoping for. Things had only progressively gotten worse since he left the store and they didn't seem to be getting any better. It seems that middle-class white folk are not prepared for the "hitting of the fan" kind of scenarios.

SUV's and soccer-mom vans were everywhere. There were plenty of people. Living people. But all of them seemed wrapped up in their own evacuations. Or busy fending off the dead. Most were making do with baseball bats, garden tools, and other small bludgeons, while a few fortunate souls even had the occasional firearm. What was once kept for home defense against a robber or intruder, was now put against an army of dead corpses. Most people did not stock ammo like that.

There was one group that caught Jeremy's attention as he peddled away from his neighborhood. It was a small group of ragtag teenagers, all wearing biohazard symbols on their clothing. He got a glimpse of one of their shirts and it read:

"ZOMBIE DEFENSE SQUAD"

The group was riding around in an old, beat-up pick-up truck, carrying anything from a machete to a crowbar. One of them, who Jeremy supposed to be the leader, held a pump-action shotgun, and wore a bandolier of shotgun shells around his chest. Jeremy watched as they jumped out into a mob of zombies and began to attack them head on.

"Go for the head!" The leader yelled.

They began to systematically smash in each of the zombies' heads. One by one, the group of corpses fell. The leader blasted the final zombie with the shotgun, sending the dead man's brains splattering against a mailbox. They all let out a yell of victory.

They were just so preoccupied with their small victory that, they didn't see the out of control truck that jumped the curb, and barreled straight for them.

Jeremy grimaced and turned his head before he could see what their outcome was, but from the screams he knew it was not good. As he neared the road he could see that cars were backed up for what looked like all the way off the island. There were really only three roads off of Wilmington Island and all ended up on Highway 80.

Being on the bike however, allowed Jeremy to very easily slip past the traffic. Horns honked, swearing filled the air, and it almost seemed like a normal traffic jam. He made his way over the bridge, crossing Turner's creek. The sun was beginning its descent into the horizon.

Maybe an hour of light left. Not much, he thought.

The tidal river and marsh seemed so peaceful. It was completely unaware of the bloodshed and the gruesome violence taking place all around it. The planet didn't seem to care that the world was falling apart. Something Jeremy had driven by so many times before now seemed to cast awe upon him. The oranges and reds burned brightly over the horizon.

He continued down Johnny Mercer Boulevard, one of the main roads leading off the islands. Cars lined the road. Looking into the cars, Jeremy could see that there was a large amount of people who tried to grab everything and take it with them. So many vehicles stuffed with "things" and barely room for people. There were those, who being smart, gathered their loved ones, and quickly left. Unfortunately, those people were stuck in the same traffic as the assholes that brought their golf clubs and 50-inch flat screen TV's.

As he peddled up to the intersection at Highway 80, the reason to why the traffic was so backed up became clear. There had been an accident. From what it looked like, it seemed that someone in a hurry, tried to run a red light, and t-boned another car, sending them careening into another. A lone ambulance was on the scene, the first emergency vehicle Jeremy had seen all afternoon. And that's saying something, seeing that he passed a *police precinct.*

Why haven't there been any cops? Or fireman? Where is all the help? He thought to himself.

He remembered *hearing* a fire truck earlier, but other than that, there had been no government vehicles all afternoon. The thought didn't make any sense, but he grew distracted with what was unfolding in front of him.

The paramedics were busy trying to resuscitate one of the victims. A white sheet covered one body on a roller-gurney. The others were still in their cars, trapped by their seatbelts. Grey smoke billowed from the hood of one of the cars. A few bystanders were trying to help and get the trapped people out.

The white sheet on the gurney stirred. The paramedics, unaware, did not notice the corpse sit up, the sheet falling off to reveal a gruesome torso wound from the accident. Something was lodged deep in the man's ribs. The medics must have deemed it a fatal wound. And normally, it would have been. But "normal" was different now. "Normal" did not mean the same thing it meant only a few hours ago.

Jeremy watched in horror as the zombie with the torso wound shambled over to the paramedics, sinking its teeth into one's neck. The victim they were trying to resuscitate revived, but not how they were used to. It quickly grabbed hold of the second paramedic and began to rip at her. The bystanders, who stopped to help, turned and saw what was happening. One froze, while the other two ran to help the medics. The one who froze began to vomit uncontrollably.

Panic. At this point, everyone else stuck in traffic saw what was happening. Cars began to bump into each other, trying to push their way out. One finally jumped a curb and pulled straight into the intersection. The driver struggled to regain control of the vehicle but instead drove straight into the helpful bystanders. More panic.

Jeremy tore his eyes away and began to peddle feverishly. There was nothing he could do. There was part of him that wanted to stay and help somehow, to help those people, but a stronger urge to stay alive kicked in. Shame began to set in as well, but he just as quickly pushed it away. There was no time for shame. He had to stay alive. His father's house was on Dutch Island, which by boat would have been maybe a five minute journey. But he didn't have a boat, he had a bicycle. So, good old fashioned roads it was then. And it was getting dark. Fast.

Chapter Four

Huge, majestic Live Oak trees were something Savannah was well known for. Their trunks could easily be the width of a full grown man and wider. The branches themselves could be trees in their own right. These trees were hundreds of years old, scattered throughout the low country. The same trees that welcomed settlers in from The Old World and that young Native American children would have played under. Spanish moss hanging from almost every inch, gently swaying in the salty breeze coming in off the marsh.

But right now, Jeremy thought. *Right now, they're blocking what little light I have left.*

It was true. The last tiny bit of light that was left as the sun finished its dip into the west was now hidden behind the massive trees. Street lights were kicking on up and down the streets.

At least there's still power.

With the rate things had been going, Jeremy almost half expected the power to go out after he said that. It didn't. He reminded himself that while it might seem like he was in some horror movie, this was unfortunately real life. And much like real life, Victory Drive was slam packed with cars.

He decided to cut through the surrounding neighborhoods and try to avoid the more main roads. Turning off Victory, he passed the gas station where every day after school he would stop with his friends and get a 69 cent fountain drink. The pumps were packed, people trying to fill up on gas and get out of town. Another advantage of the bike was not having to worry about fuel. The thought almost brought a smile to Jeremy's face, except he would need a certain type of "fuel" soon. Food.

Continuing down the road, he passed his old high school, Johnson High. He slowed down, taking in the school for what could be the last time. Jeremy didn't really like or dislike his high school experience. He was not one of those people who looked back on the "glory days," but at the same time there was a small part of him that missed the simplicity of life then. Graduating for Jeremy meant growing up quickly. While most of his friends went off to a distant college or other adventures, Jeremy was stuck in Savannah working. All of that was long gone now.

"Cutting through Savannah State would make the most sense, I can get to La Roche from there, and that'll take me straight to Dad's," he said, working it out loud as he went.

When he got to the college, he expected the worst. But in reality, it looked abandoned. Which was strange, seeing that it was the middle of the semester. He saw a few corpses wandering around, but other than that, the place was a ghost town.

Maybe everybody got out of here in time. It is a Thursday. They could just be all gone.

That was what he hoped. The dead there did not look like college students. More like they wandered in from the surrounding neighborhoods. One stood out in particular.

It, he, whatever it was now, was an older man, maybe mid-fifties. He was wearing patterned pajama pants, a white tank top, and a dark colored robe. He shuffled around in his slippers. This man was just going about his normal evening routine, and then BAM! Zombie apocalypse. The thought began to creep into Jeremy's mind that things will never be the same again.

Maybe the Government will figure out a cure or fix this somehow, but for a lot of people, this was going to a have a lasting impact. You will never forget the time when your loved ones tried to eat you in your living room. Or the time you saw your mother torn to pieces.

Jeremy tried to push the thought from his mind. Too many thoughts, too much thinking. It was all too deep and dark to dwell on right now. He had to focus. He made his way safely through the college without confrontation and found himself on the road he was aiming for. The sun was completely set now, street lights the only present source of illumination. The darkness made Jeremy nervous. He pressed on. There was large Baptist church to his right. He'd never been there, but his mother only had kind things to say about it. She didn't attend there herself, but had gone to some of their special events.

Again, all of that was suddenly thrust into the past. How quickly the present evaporated into the past. Jeremy shook his head. He had to refocus; all of this thinking was taking him off the task at hand. And that was finding his father. And staying alive. He didn't really care for his father, but he was family, and all Jeremy had left now. That is, if the man was still alive.

With all the thinking that he was doing, Jeremy didn't notice the large group of zombies in front of him in the middle of the road. They saw him however and began to hobble in his direction. It was then that he noticed them noticing him and he brought the bike to a screeching halt. It was too much of a sudden stop, because with the weight of the backpack, it sent him spilling over the handlebars, and dumping the bike. It slid out behind him, putting him in between the zombies and the bike.

Jeremy hit the ground hard. As he came to a rolling stop, he winced through the pain, and tried to do a quick head count.

Five, no, six of them. There were six of them.

All moaning and jawing towards him. He had taken on three of them, but this was twice that many, and he was not feeling the same surge of adrenaline he had felt then. The rage. This time he only felt fear.

Jeremy ran in the direction of the church, leaving the bike, because the dead were gaining on him. Maybe he could get inside and barricade himself in. It was just like the horror movies this time. This was the scene where the girl was running away from the monster, and no matter how fast she ran away, the monster somehow seemed to catch up. Jeremy was the girl.

There was a rather tall, iron gate surrounding the church property. Every ten to fifteen feet, there would be a large brick column, and then more iron fence. The tops of the iron bars were tipped with sharp looking ends.

Yes, that screams friendly, he thought.

Whatever the purpose for the large gate, it did not change the fact that he was smack dab between the iron fence and a large group of things that only wanted to devour him.

Talk about a rock and hard place, his sarcasm whispered.

There was no way he could fit between the bars; they were too narrow. And there was no way he was jumping that thing. He ran along the side of the fence, hoping to find an opening or a gate or something that would let him get through. Nothing. And then Jeremy did the worst thing possible.

He tripped.

"You've got to be fucking kidding me! Is this a movie?!" he yelled.

A lone zombie had pulled ahead of the pack. His decomposing legs must have been a little fresher than the others. Very quickly, he was on top of Jeremy. When he fell, the corpse lurched forward and grabbed the boy. Jeremy held it off; its jaw's drooling and snapping back and forth. Back and forth. The drool was cold and thick. He pushed the thing away from him as far as he could, noticing that the others were getting closer.

BOOM!

The zombie's head exploded into a splash of cerebral mass and goo. Jeremy looked up towards the fence and saw the figure of a man standing there, the business end of the shotgun pointed where the zombie's head once was.

"RUN HIJO! KEEP TO THE FENCE AND I'LL COVER YOU!" the man yelled.

Jeremy didn't hesitate. He threw the headless body off and scrambled to his feet, breaking out into a full sprint along the fence. He heard another blast from the shotgun and a thud. Another zombie fell.

Four left, he counted in his head.

He did not dare turn to count, but continued to run full speed. His days in cross-country were beginning to pay off. His breathing became steady and focused.

"A LITTLE FURTHER AND THERE'S THE GATE!"

Jeremy began to feel his lungs burn and his legs ache. It had been a while since he ran this intensely. He did not have much more to give. A few more feet. Another blast behind him. He reached the gate and flung it open. As soon as he was inside, the man slammed the gate shut and threw a chain around it. He then locked it with a keyed lock. The last three zombies clawed through the iron fence, the chain holding the gate shut. They could not get through.

"Quick. Follow me," the man commanded sharply.

Jeremy did not argue with him. The man led him up to a smaller church building and to a door that had been boarded up with plywood. After they entered, the man turned and locked the door behind them. They went up some stairs and into what looked like the office of one of the pastors. There was a small, wooden desk with two arm chairs sitting in front of it and a small, well-used couch against the far wall. The man again closed the door behind them and locked the door.

Jeremy watched as the man walked across the room to the window and began to peer out through the blinds. He was dressed in all black. Black slacks and a black dress shirt. He was also wearing a white collar around his neck.

The man was a priest.

Chapter Five

"Thank you," Jeremy finally managed to vocalize.

The man nodded. He wasn't giving Jeremy his full attention yet, still peering out the window. Seeing the man now in a fuller light, Jeremy noticed the brownish tinge of the man's skin. His face was weathered, especially for a man who seemed to be in his mid-forties.

"Are you a priest?" Jeremy asked bluntly.

The man barely nodded, still continuing to stare out the window.

"I thought this was a Baptist church?"

"It is, was," the man answered. "I don't work here hijo. I came to the city to visit friends when this all began to happen. This was the closest church that looked open. I was hoping to seek refuge with some hermanos, some brothers, regardless of our particular faiths. Jesus is still our God."

The man's Spanish accent was much thicker in this longer section of speech. It had not been as noticeable when he was barking commands and Jeremy was running for his life.

"Uh, ok. Um... Father, uh, Padre," Jeremy stammered. "Any idea what the hell is going on here?"

The Padre looked away from the window, a sly grin forming around his lips. He seemed to ponder Jeremy's question before finally answering.

"I think you have answered your own question. Hell is going on here."

Is this guy for real? Jeremy thought.

The Padre's grin faded and he looked back to the window. After a few minutes of awkward silence passed, the Padre pushed the blinds back towards the window and turned his full attention to Jeremy. The boy was visibly shaken.

He did just survive a pretty close call with those monsters. If I hadn't made it to the gate in time, he would probably be dead right now, thought the man.

"What is your name, hijo?" the Padre asked, clearing his throat.

"Jeremy."

"Well, Jeremy," the priest started. "You are very fortunate to be alive right now."

Jeremy snapped out of his daze and looked the priest in the eyes.

"Fortunate?" he retorted. "Please enlighten me, Padre, on how I am 'fortunate'? I saw my mother get torn apart by those crazy people, I've had to kill several of those people today, and I almost fu-freaking died out there a few minutes ago!"

The priest moved away from the window and slowly walked up to Jeremy, as if to walk up on a wounded animal. He gently placed his hands on the boy's shoulders and smiled.

"You are alive, hijo. For that you should be grateful. Not many people have survived the day's events. I am sorry for the loss of your mother. I am. Many terrible things have been done today, but your mother, I know she would want you to be grateful for your life," the man said calmly and smoothly.

Jeremy knew he was right. And he was glad to be alive. He just didn't know how to handle all of this. People freak out when they lose loved ones in normal situations. Watching dead people fight over and rip apart your mother's body was not a normal situation.

"I tried to save her..." Jeremy choked out, tears beginning to slide down his cheeks.

His emotions were beginning to take control of him. He had cried at the house earlier, but those tears were different. Earlier, all he felt was anger and the rage. But it was just now hitting him he would never see his mom again. She believed in heaven, but Jeremy always thought that was just wishful thinking.

You just die, he thought.

And besides, if how she believed you got there was true, then Jeremy definitely would not be seeing her again. Too much bad stuff in his life. Too much anger towards God. And believing that some man two thousand years ago died for his sins? That was too much for Jeremy. He played around with the idea when he was younger, but as he grew older, it became harder to believe in that.

"I'm sure you did try to save her, hijo," the Padre said. "Sometimes the circumstances are beyond our control and we have to trust in Go-"

"Yeah? And where was God in all this?" Jeremy angrily cut him off. "Where was God when I was trying to save her? Where is he now Padre? Huh? What's he up to right now? Just chillin up there in the sky, watchin the show?"

The Padre took his hands off of Jeremy's shoulders as the boy ranted. He very casually leaned back against the desk and listened.

"I mean, what is all of this?" Jeremy continued. "Some sort of sick cosmical joke? 'Let's watch those humans eat each other.' Yeah, good one God! Very funny! 'Let's watch Jeremy try and save his mother, only to fail and let her die.' What kind of sick prick would do that? Huh, Padre? Where is your God now?"

The man just watched as Jeremy flipped his lid. His expression was set; his face never changing. There was a hint of sadness in his face as he patiently listened to the boy's lament.

"You finished hijo?"

He asked very calmly. His calmness was in stark contrast with Jeremy's off the cuff frustration. This only added to Jeremy's frustration.

"Hijo? What does that even mean anyways?" Jeremy barked.

The man smiled.

"Sorry," he started. "It's Spanish for 'son'. You can take the priest out of México, but you can't take the México out of the priest."

Jeremy quickly grew embarrassed. If he had calmed down and thought clearly, he would have remembered that from Spanish class. A class which he actually did well in. His head hung low. The priest paused for minute, processing all of what Jeremy said.

"To be honest with you hijo," Padre began. "I don't fully understand what is going on here. I don't know how this all came to be. But I do know one thing: God is good. And loving. This disease or whatever it is making people act this way, this is just me thinking, but I have a hard time believing it is from God. Too many times has man tried to play God and met disastrous results. This, this reeks of that. I don't think this plague is from God, but yet more likely, God has allowed it to happen."

"Yeah," Jeremy said. "Well, why would He just allow this to happen then? That doesn't seem very loving or good."

"God works in mysterious ways. I know that has become quite the cliché here in the states, but that doesn't change the fact that the statement still rings true. He could have very easily stopped all of this. Without breaking a sweat. Do you honestly believe that an all-powerful God couldn't stop this? Easily he could. I don't know why He allows certain things to happen. But I do know the book of Romans tells us that He allows us to pursue after the lusts in our hearts and He turns us over to our debased minds. In a sense, God says, 'Fine, if sin is all you want, then go get it. Go chase the wind.' It may sound harsh, but he does that because he loves us. He wants us to know that we can chase things all day, money, sex, but in the end, we will be incomplete without him."

Jeremy nodded slowly, digesting every word the Padre said. Flashes of old felt-board, Sunday School lessons came to mind.

"Also, it says in Ephesians, that we are dead in our trespasses and sins. We think we are alive, but in reality we are spiritually dead. Sound familiar? These things out there, they are not so much different from us. I'm not saying that God allowed this to happen to teach us that, but you have to admit the irony is amazing."

Jeremy again nods.

"You see, Jeremy," he said. "These dead are a great picture of us. We are dead and our only desire is to consume, no matter what the cost. For us it can be anything, money, fame, or even good things. But for these dead, it is flesh. And they will consume it no matter what the cost. We have all rebelled against God and pursued His creations more than Him. We have desired the creation over the Creator. And then we have the audacity to say that He owes us! That God is unfair! God owes no man! Everything in the universe is His! We stand there and point our fingers to the heavens and say, 'Where are you God? Why have you done this to me?' When all the while we are the ones running and rebelling against Him, the One who created us and gave us breath."

The Padre stopped. He did not mean to preach to the boy, but something moved him to say all this. Maybe it was frustration, maybe it was concern. Or maybe, maybe he was preaching this to himself. Reminding himself of the truth he knew to be true.

"Jeremy," he said, taking a deep breath before starting again.

"Everyone wants to blame God for when the world falls apart. Never stopping to think that maybe it's us who are tearing it apart and it is Him who is holding it all together."

The words hung in the air as Jeremy let them sink in. Ever since his parents divorced, he had held a chip on his shoulder when it came to God. But if what the priest was saying was true, then maybe it wasn't God's fault for his parent's failed marriage. Maybe, it was just theirs.

"So," Jeremy began, still working out what he was going to say in response. "Then God is just gonna leave us here to our own devices? He's just gonna leave us here with these freaks? Just let us destroy ourselves? Or I guess now, eat ourselves?"

He noticed the man light up and a big, warm smile crossed his face.

"No, hijo!" Padre said, beaming. "That's nowhere near the end of the story! The Father has set in motion a plan of redemption for us long before the creation of the world…"

There was a crash from downstairs.

Both men's heads snapped in the direction of the door. The Padre held up a finger to his mouth, signaling to Jeremy for silence. He received no argument as Jeremy froze. He reached over to the desk and picked the shotgun up, slowly and quietly. There was shuffling and other noises heard from the other side of the door.

"Hijo," the Padre whispered.

Jeremy turned to look at the priest. He was holding out a set of keys.

"There is a small, blue pick-up truck in the parking lot. Use it to escape."

"But what about you? Where are you going?" Jeremy stammered.

But it was too late. The Padre had already flung

open the door and started firing into the crowd of zombies.

Chapter Six

Boom. Splat. Boom. Splat.

The Padre laid out the dead with a steady rhythm of shotgun shells and brain matter. How a group that size got into the building without alerting them both was beyond Jeremy. Perhaps he was so focused on what the Padre was saying and the Padre was so enwrapped in saying it, that the two of them had simply just missed the noise. It was almost as if the zombies had snuck in.

Boom. Splat. Boom. Splat. Click. Click. Click.

Padre's gun was out of shells, but that didn't stop the priest from his attack. He took the butt end of the gun and swung it into the head of a girl whose left eye was hanging from the socket. The blow threw her head back and the eye flew off into the crowd.

"Hijo! You need to run now!" Padre yelled.

Jeremy realized that he had frozen to watch the man of God deal a massive blow to the dead onslaught. He moved with such speed and precision. For a man who was called to peace and love, he moved like a trained warrior. Jeremy watched as the man connected a fist with the face of zombie, sending the thing recoiling back into the group, clearing a path. It was time to run.

Jeremy pulled the machete out from his backpack and ran into the fray. The Padre had cleared the path down the stairs, but Jeremy would have to hack and slash his way through to make the path wide enough for him to slip by. He did, as the Padre followed behind him, pushing the boy forward. They fought their way down the stairs and into the reception area. Jeremy was just about to open the door, when a zombie hand reached out and grabbed him by his backpack. He spun quickly, fixing to bring the machete down on the rotting arm, but watched as the butt end of the shotgun came crashing down onto its skull.

"Run for the truck," the winded man said.

Jeremy did. His feet hit the asphalt and took off in the direction of the blue pickup. The herd of zombies outside was larger than the one inside. The gunfire from earlier must have attracted them to the church, because it was quickly being overrun. How they were getting in around the fences was a mystery to Jeremy. There must have been an opening somewhere. Jeremy looked towards the truck and counted five zombies in between him and his escape.

No biggie, he thought.

He ran with all he had, refreshed from the short break. His backpack bounced against his back, propelling him forward. He zipped past the first zombie with no problem. It was slow. He turned to see if the Padre was behind him. He was not.

"Where is he?" he asked out loud.

There was a small group of dead massing near the door; some were kneeling down over something. One of them stood up. It was holding something near to its mouth. Jeremy squinted, trying to make out what it was. It was a blood stained white collar.

"No!" he yelled.

The dead in unison all looked at him, losing interest in the meal they had before them. They were now setting their sights on something new to consume. One moaned, thus causing the others to moan in reply as they shambled in Jeremy's direction.

He turned and began to run towards the truck, but came face to face with one of the living dead. Its eyes were grey and dull, void of any life. The smell of decomposing flesh filled Jeremy's nostrils; he would have thrown up, but the danger was too imminent. Its wilted arms reached out, not for a friendly hug, but trying to grab a hold of its prey. Jeremy swung the machete up into the air and then brought the full force of it crashing back down onto the zombie's skull.

Its grey, dead eyes rolled back into its head, thick, brown blood pouring from where the blade split through bone and tissue. Jeremy went to yank the blade back. It didn't budge. It was stuck. He tried again. Stuck. The other dead approached quickly.

Fuck it, he thought and ran, pushing over the zombie who stole his only weapon.

When he got to the truck, he did not become the girl from the movies again. He did not fiddle with his keys and drop them over and over again. He got in, slid them into the ignition, and roared the truck to life. The brights came on when he cranked the truck on. The dead did not seem to like the sudden change of light, because all caught in the beams of the truck threw up their arms, shielding themselves from the light. The dead do not like the light.

Jeremy threw the truck into drive and floored it. He took out one of the zombies in the process, sending its dead body tumbling under the pick-up. As he drove towards the exit, he saw what looked like the Padre's lifeless body still lying over by the building. For being mostly intact, he still had not gone through the transformation into one of those things. He was still dead.

He should be up by now. They have been coming back quicker than that. Maybe some take longer.

Jeremy turned his attention back to driving. He reached the exit gate, ran out and swung open the large gate. Quickly, he returned to the truck as the dead were trying to catch up to him across the parking lot. He pulled the truck out onto the street and took off in the direction of his father's house. The roads were eerily clear of any traffic. The problem was the abandoned vehicles. They were everywhere. Savannah streets could be narrow enough, but add derelict cars to the equation, and you were looking at a tight squeeze. It was like people tried to leave, but just abandoned their vehicles and made off on foot. He swiftly, but carefully guided the truck down the road.

As he came a few blocks short of the neighborhood his father lived in, the blocked roadways became too clogged for the truck to get through. He was going to have to make the rest of his journey on foot. Now the reason for all the abandoned cars was beginning to make sense. He did not like the idea of walking. Especially, since he didn't have his machete anymore, but what choice did he have?

Looking around to see if he could find anything in the cab that would be of some use, he came across the Padre's bible. Much like his mother's, the cover was cracked and worn, the pages creased and nearly falling out. Page after page was filled with markings and notes. This book had seen much use.

"I already have Mom's," he said, setting the book down on the seat.

He picked up another book, a worn, leather covered notebook. He flipped it open to see handwritten pages crammed full of tiny writing, both in English and Spanish. It was the Padre's journal. Now that the Padre was gone, Jeremy could still get to know the man through his journal. He decided to read it later, tucking the book into his bag, next to his Mother's bible. A last quick scan of the truck and the only thing he found to replace his machete was a Phillips head screwdriver.

Better than nothing I guess.

He quietly closed the door and began to walk towards his father's house. The street lights were still on. This area still had power. This somewhat comforted Jeremy. The shadows the light cast across the road, however, did not. They played tricks on Jeremy's eyes. Every dark corner seemed to hiding a zombie. They might have been.

Normally, you would need to have a pass to enter

the gated community, but today, the gates were wide open. One of them hung broken from its hinges. The guard shack was abandoned and the light was still on inside. Jeremy gripped the screwdriver tight to his chest. He had to be ready for anything. If those things could sneak up on him and the Padre at the church, very easily one of them could get the jump on him here.

It was empty. He breathed a sigh of relief. Jeremy felt himself getting tired and he needed to rest. The whole incident at the church was beginning to take its toll on him, the adrenaline not pumping in him as it wasthen. Plus, he was getting hungry.

What was the last thing I ate?

It was an energy drink and a bag of chips on his break at work.

Work... I guess I don't have to go back to that place.

He began to think about the shopping carts. He thought about Brian the douche yelling at him about the shopping carts. He thought about Ashley, giggling at him as he struggled with the shopping carts.

Ash...

She was probably the only reason he still worked there. He had thought of quitting several times, but the fact that she was there, made him stay. And he never worked up the courage to ask her out. They had talked several times, shared their breaks together, and she probably even considered him a friend. There was one time when Brian was being extra-douchey to everyone and was yelling at Ashley for something. Jeremy brought up the fact that he messed up one woman's coupons just to take the heat off Ashley. Brian fell for the bait and ever since, Ashley had been nice to Jeremy.

Until now, he thought. *She's dead. Brian's dead. Mom and the Padre are all dead.*

There were no dead here. It seemed that these rich

people made it out alive. Four car garages were left open. Light in 14,000+ square feet houses were still on. Some of these houses were on deep water. Jeremy wondered if anybody tried to escape by boat.

Not a bad idea, he thought. *Except that you would have to return to land eventually to get food and drinkable water. On second thought, maybe not such a good idea.*

He reached his destination without any problems. The lights were not on in the house. Looking at his cell phone, he discovered the screen had cracked.

Probably when I flew off the bike.

It was still readable though. It was only 11:17. It had been seven hours since Jeremy was at work. Much had changed in seven hours.

The house was empty. It looked like his father wasn't here. Normal.

"Hello?" Jeremy called out into the darkness. "Dad? You home?"

There was no answer. No moans either, so he pressed on into the house. He flipped on a few light switches, his eyes taking some time to adjust from coming in out of the dark. The house was clean and in order. It didn't even look like someone lived here. Jeremy wandered up to his father's bedroom, turning on lights as he went.

The master bedroom was also empty and very clean. The bed was made, clothes were off the floor and put away. This wasn't like his dad. The man lived his life like the extravagant bachelor he was. After the divorce, his father won a huge pile of money in Vegas. So, on top of the man's money as a plastic surgeon, he now had a few million more. Meanwhile, Jeremy's mother was left working two jobs and other side work just to keep the bills paid. Even Jeremy would pitch in from his paycheck.

His mother wanted nothing to do with his father, so

she wouldn't accept a dime from the man. Jeremy didn't care for the man either, but he wouldn't have minded having a little of the man's cash. Birthdays were normally nice. They were one of the few times his mother allowed him to accept money from his father.

The only thing that seemed out of place in the room was a video camera set up on a tripod. It was pointed directly at the bed.

Probably don't want to see what's on that thing, he thought with a grimace.

His father always had some new piece of arm-candy that was more attracted to the man's financial status than his personality. His father was probably a close second to Brian in doucheness. Being a plastic surgeon, the man had his options of "female companionship." Just one more reason Jeremy disliked his father. He left the room and headed towards the kitchen. His stomach was growling. He had to get something to eat.

Once in the kitchen, he went straight to the fridge. It was as empty as the house. There was an expired gallon of milk, a few slices of moldy cheese, and a lone yogurt shoved in the back. Jeremy grabbed the yogurt and closed the door.

Please be good, please be good...

He looked at the expiration date. It still had a few weeks left. He began to frantically search through the drawers for a spoon. After not finding one, he ripped the lid off the yogurt, and crushed the cup, the yogurt erupting into his mouth.

Sweet Jesus. That is some good yogurt. I don't even care how stupid I look right now.

He wasn't sure if the yogurt was really good or that he was just so stinking hungry. He finished it and threw the cup into the sink. Wiping off the yogurt from around his mouth, he noticed a picture sitting on the counter.

It was a picture of him and his father.

That's new. I've never seen that before. It might even be the only picture of me in this place.

They looked happier in the picture. Jeremy was wearing a baseball uniform, holding his glove and a baseball. His father stood next to him, beaming with pride. Jeremy remembered that day. It was the day his little league team won the championship. His dad was the coach then. That was before the divorce. Frustration washed over Jeremy's face.

Why? Why did you have to mess everything up?

He took the frame and placed it face down on the counter. It was then that he noticed the piece of paper sitting on the counter next to the frame. It was a note to the cleaning ladies. Apparently, Jeremy's father wasn't even in town. He wasn't even in the country. He was off on a pleasure cruise in the middle of the ocean on his private yacht. The world has gone to hell and where was his father? Living it up out on the ocean.

"That son of a bi-," Jeremy started, but stopped when he saw a picture of his Grandmother on the kitchen wall. She seemed to be looking down on him, with disapproving eyes towards his foul language.

"Sorry Grandma."

He crumpled up the note and threw it across the room. His mother was dead and his father was nowhere to be found. This made Jeremy so much more exhausted. Wandering into the living room, he collapsed onto the couch. His eyes were growing heavy with sleep.

"I just wish this day was over," he whispered.

He was just about to doze off when he heard gun shots coming from outside.

Chapter Seven

The sleep vanished as Jeremy jumped up to his feet. He ran over to the window, to try and see what was going on outside. From where he was positioned in the house, he could only see a large pickup truck. It was one of those jacked up, big mud tire, bubba-kinda trucks. From what he could make out, there was one bubba in the driver's seat and two others standing in the bed of the truck. The two in the back were both holding guns. Jeremy was fairly confident that the one driving probably had a gun on him too.

He moved to the front door to get a better look.

Maybe they're hunting zombies.

Hunting zombies. The thought sent shivers down Jeremy's spine.

Is that how it's gonna be? No longer are people going to hunt animals for sport, but the living dead?

The thought was sick. But at least they were getting rid of them. Making it safer. He wasn't sure if it was that thought that made him go outside or the fact that they were living people. Actual living people. What was he going to do? Tell the living people to leave the living dead people alone? He had already killed several of them, who was he to tell them not to?

As he stepped outside though, he realized that they were not after zombies. Hiding and crouched down behind a car was a single black man.

"Hey nigger," one yelled. "We got sumthin' to tell you."

"Yeah boy," the other chimed in. "Come on out now. We can do this all civilized. Or not."

The two men laughed as Jeremy watched on in horror.

"Hey boy! My buddy's talkin' to you!" the first one yelled.

Jeremy could see that Bubba #1 was holding a hunting rifle in one hand and a half-empty bottle of bourbon in the other. Not a good combination for a bunch of racist hicks. These were the kinda guys that gave southerners a bad name as dumb, white-trash rednecks.

The guy behind the car did not budge and Jeremy didn't blame him. He knew they didn't want to just "talk." Bubba #2 was holding a camouflaged shotgun. Things could go very badly, very quickly. So, Jeremy did what any sane person would do in that situation.

"Hey! What do you think you're doing?" he shouted.

The words spilled out of his mouth before he could even think of an appropriate response. The three bubbas and even the guy behind the car all looked at Jeremy as if he was the crazy one.

Tough crowd.

"Go back inside rich boy," Bubba #1 said. "This don't concern you."

"I don't live here," Jeremy answered. "Why don't y'all leave him alone?"

He thickened his accent a little to try and create a language bridge between them. It seemed to work as they pondered it for a moment. But Jeremy realized these were not the bridge building type of men when Bubba #2 pumped a round into his weapon.

"Don't think we'll be doin' that. Now go on and git back inside. Go on now," he said very calmly.

It was the unsettling kind of calm. The kind you feel right before some serious doo doo is about to hit the fan. Jeremy looked over to the black guy. The guy looked directly back at him.

"Just go," the man mouthed.

It was at that point where Jeremy began to feel the rage build back up in him. The same rage he felt at the supermarket and in his driveway. This was not right.

He could not let them do this. The rage began to seep into his bloodstream, his muscles tightening, and his jaw clenched.

Zombie apocalypse or not, this is wrong.

The only problem was this: they had guns. He had a screwdriver.

Screw it.

"Y'all are gonna have to leave. Now," Jeremy said, just as calmly as Bubba #1 had.

Bubba #2 fired his gun into the warm night's air. All three men began to let out whoops and hollers. Bubba #1 took a swig from the bourbon.

"Woo doggie! This boy has some balls," he yelled out.

And that was when they heard the moans.

Oh, shit...

The gunshots and noise had attracted the dead. Moans and groans came from every direction. Perhaps the neighborhood was not as empty as Jeremy had thought. The bubbas were locking and loading, getting ready for the oncoming dead attack. Driver Bubba got out of the truck and was holding some kind of long barreled revolver. Jeremy noticed the guy behind the car start to stand up from his hiding spot, but still staying low enough to the ground in case the rednecks turned their attention back to him.

The first of the zombies began to shamble out from every direction. Ten of them, easy. And more were beginning to trickle in. Jeremy was right. This neighborhood was not empty at all.

"Alright boys," Bubba #1 shouted to his friends. "Let's kill sum zombies!"

Before they could fire a shot, a new sound filled the night. Not a moan or grunt that was accustomed to the living dead, but this time a piercing shriek. It was a higher pitch, raspy, and sounded forced through decaying vocal cords. This was something else. This knew it was the runners, which is what he was calling the new type of zombie, because of the screams. Not moans. He almost missed the moans. Others began to beat on the door. The wooden door cracked. It was not going to last long.

"We have to get out of here," Ben said. "Is there a safe back door?"

Jeremy motioned towards the kitchen.

"Through the kitchen. The garage."

Ben nodded and motioned with his head that they should get going. They quickly moved through the kitchen, Jeremy only stopping to grab his father's keys off the counter.

When they got to the garage, it was dark. Jeremy went to turn on the lights but Ben stopped him. He shook his head and pulled out something from his pocket. It was lighter. He flicked it on and the small flame gave them enough light to see why Jeremy stopped to grab the keys. His father's Jeep.

Another one of his father's many toys. A brand new, four-door, jet black Jeep Wrangler. And just like its owner, it was fully loaded with a bunch of crap. They both got in and buckled up. Safety first.

"What size shoe do you wear?" Jeremy asked.

"What? Why?"

Jeremy reached into the back seat and pulled out his father's gym duffle bag. He pulled out a pair of practically new running shoes. His dad probably used them twice.

"These are an eleven. Will that work for you?"

Ben nodded and took the shoes, quickly putting them on.

"Ready?" Jeremy asked.

"As ready as I can be," Ben replied.

Jeremy hit the garage door opener. As soon as the door cleared, Jeremy threw it in reverse and backed out into the drive. A few shamblers were on the driveway, but no runners. Jeremy began to drive towards the street. He swerved around the first zombie, but nicked the second. It let out a moan as the Jeep bumped it. It was answered with shrieks. The runners noticed the Jeep. There were two of them and they broke out into full sprint towards the Jeep.

"Go! Go! Go!" Ben screamed.

Jeremy floored it and hit the third zombie head on. Speed bump. He took off down the street, the runners trailing behind. Something else grabbed their attention and they took off down another street. Ben let out a deep breath.

"Sweet Jesus," he said.

Chapter Eight

The two men rode in silence as they passed through the neighborhoods leading into town. The appearance of this new type of zombie had really shaken them. As if the slow, dumb shamblers weren't dangerous enough, now you have these dead, free running freaks to deal with. Both men knew the odds were now greatly stacked against them.

Before, they could just have been avoided, or at least out smarted, Jeremy thought. *But now these crazy mofos? This is not good...*

The future did seem bleaker. They had no weapons to defend themselves against these runners, with the exception of Jeremy's screwdriver. And he did not want to get close enough to use that thing.

"We're going to need to find some kind of weapons," Jeremy said, breaking the silence.

"Yeah," Ben replied. "I had a baseball bat, but I lost it when I was running from those deranged rednecks."

"I had a machete. Got stuck in a zombie's head."

"Zombies?" Ben asked. "You mean like in the movies?"

"Yeah, that's what these things are right?" Jeremy asked in reply. "I mean, they sure do act like them. I haven't seen many zombie movies, never really was into that kinda stuff, but dead coming back to life and eating the living? That seems like zombies to me."

Ben shook his head.

"But those are the movies man. Fiction. This can't be real," he said.

Jeremy did not know what to think. He hadn't really had a chance to stop and think about it. If these things were not zombies, then what were they? Sick people? If they were just sick people, then when Jeremy killed them... He couldn't think about that.

"Whatever they are, we are going to need something to defend ourselves. Especially if there's more of those crazy, jumper ones," Jeremy said.

"Yeah. What were those?" Ben asked.

"I don't know. Maybe there's different types of zombies. Or maybe they're evolving or something."

"Alright, so where do we go?" Ben said, nodding. "I can tell you that any local gun shop will be crawling with rednecks. And if it's not, then it's empty. Just trust me on that one."

"Is that where you ran into those guys?" Jeremy asked.

"Yeah. Apparently, there are too many black people with guns and they thought they'd even it out. You know how many *niggers* were there? One. Me."

Jeremy could only shake his head. One of the great things about the South. Where the racism wasn't blatantly obvious, it was quietly lurking in the shadows.

"You have to be careful on *that* side of town."

"What is wrong with *those* people?"

Jeremy had heard it all. Especially the older white women on the island. They had no problem with sharing their opinions on everything. But rednecks, man, you gotta love the rednecks. It was like they were trapped in their own little country-bumpkin world. And what drove Jeremy insane was that so many people chose to live that way. There were kids at school who would act all backwoods, but he knew they lived on the islands, in houses on deep water. It just made no sense to him. To be fair though, it was not as if just white people were the only racist ones. Everybody was kind of racist in the South.

"Can I tell you something," Ben said, interrupting Jeremy's thoughts on racism in the South. "I'm adopted. You know by who? White folks. Yup. Man, I grew up in the country! I was probably more country than those rednecks! I didn't grow up in no ghetto, listening to gangsta rap and drinking forties. I grew up out past Rincon, listening to George Jones and Skynyrd, and drinking sweet ass tea!"

"Ass tea?" Jeremy asked with a coy smile. "That sounds gross."

Ben looked at the 19 year old with a brief dumbfounded look, but then cracked a smile, and both men burst into laughing. They laughed for a good minute, something they had not done in a while. It felt good to laugh. Everything was beginning to seem so bleak; it was nice to know that there were still some funny things in the world. Like "ass tea."

Jeremy stopped when they got to Montgomery Crossroads. If it was clear of any traffic it would give them a straight shot across Savannah's Southside. As far as he could see in the dark, it looked clear. Maybe they would get lucky. But Jeremy knew that they would have to be extremely lucky to get across town with no problems.

There was a Super Wal-Mart not far from where they were. If there was something they needed, then that was the place they would find it.

"How about Wally World?" Jeremy asked.

"You don't hunt much do you?"

"No, but I play a lot of paintball."

The older man chuckled at this.

"Paintball, huh? Well, I don't know how paintballs are selling nowadays, but gun ammo is scarce. Especially at ol' Wally World. And that was before all of this happened."

"Oh," Jeremy said. "I didn't know."

"Yeah, when our government started cracking down on guns, ammo sales went through the roof, and the demand quickly swallowed up the supply. We might not find any guns there either. But maybe we'll find something else. Like tools or something. Let's try it."

Jeremy nodded and put the Jeep back in drive. The thought of finding a replacement machete was on Jeremy's mind. It would be nice to have one that wasn't covered in rust too. There would also be food there. That yogurt did absolutely nothing for him. All this running around and bashing people's heads in was beginning to wear on Jeremy physically. His body ached.

Turning into the parking lot, they both realized they made a huge error. The first thing that caught their eyes was that the building was on fire. Not a good sign. The view of the building from the road had been blocked by the trees, and in the dark of night; they did not see the smoke billowing from the rooftop.

The second thing that caught their attention was the large crowd of dead standing in the parking lot. There must have been twenty-something of them standing there. All of them had their arms up blocking the light from the fire, but yet they all lacked the common sense to walk away from it. Whatever little common sense this group of people once had, was now long gone out the window.

"I think we should probably go somewhere else," Ben said.

"I think you are on to something," Jeremy replied.

He began to back the Jeep back down the road they drove in on. Ben motioned towards the lights, and Jeremy quickly shut them off in order to not attract any unwanted attention. Once back out on the road, he turned them back on and they slowly made their way down Montgomery Crossroads.

The street lights were still on in this area as well, so that must have meant there was still power here too. Jeremy assumed it would be a matter of time before the power did shut off, but he was thankful for it while they had it. More than likely, the workers at the power plants and Power Company would care more about their own families and not so much about keeping the electricity pumping.

"There. That hardware store," Ben said, pointing off to the left.

There was a small, locally owned hardware store. It looked vacant and there were no visible zombies around. Of course, that did not mean that there wasn't any lurking around in the shadows. Jeremy pulled the Jeep into the store's parking lot and shut the engine off. It was quiet.

"Do you think it's safe?" Jeremy asked.

"I don't know," Ben answered. "Looks empty. And I don't see any dead. I doubt that a store like that has firearms, but maybe we can find some tools to use as weapons."

He paused and then smiled.

"Anything would be better than what we have now."

Jeremy nodded. He too didn't like the idea of having no protection, especially with those crazy freaks running around now. He reached for the door handle and slowly opened it. There was a faint click. No zombies. Ben reached for his handle and just as slowly opened it.

They both walked up to the store, watching over their shoulders. The windows had been boarded up, but you could see light escaping through the cracks. Power was still on in the store. Whether or not anybody was inside was another thing.

Jeremy reached out for the door and looked to Ben. Ben nodded and Jeremy proceeded to pull open the door. It was unlocked. They both stepped in, pulling the door shut behind them. Ben quickly locked it and then he gave Jeremy a nod.

"Hello?" Jeremy called out, his voice loud enough for someone to hear him, but still quiet enough to not draw any unwanted attention from outside.

"Is anybody in here?"

Please don't answer.

Only silence. The men looked at each other and seemed to "telepathically" say, "It's clear." Sighs of relief. Jeremy really was not ready for another fight. He was tired. And hungry. Maybe there would be some beef jerky somewhere. Anything sounded appetizing right now.

As he wandered off down one of the aisles, the first item that looked like a good weapon was a crowbar. Black iron and heavy, he was sure the claw end could do some damage if needed. He gave it a practice swing and grinned.

It'll do.

Meanwhile, Ben was picking up a simple claw hammer. His tool's claw was similar to Jeremy's, yet not as heavy and much more maneuverable. If anything popped out, he would be ready to bring that claw down on its skull. When he reached the end of the aisle, Jeremy was standing there with crowbar in hand.

"Let's make sure the building is clear first and then we'll go shopping," Ben said.

They walked around the perimeter of the aisles, carefully looking down each one. When they came full circle, another sigh of relief was given. The store was empty.

"Alright, let's go shopping!" an excited Ben said.

"Heck yeah. I saw a new machete to replace my old one. It didn't even have any rust on it!" Jeremy answered.

The grown men took off like kids in the candy store. After a few minutes, they both returned back up front, goodies in tow. Jeremy found a garden buggy and filled it with his loot. Ben walked back up with hands full.

"Oh, buggy was a good choice," Ben said upon seeing Jeremy's little red wagon.

"Yup. I like to be resourceful," Jeremy said with a grin.

"Well, what do you think about this then?" Ben asked, holding up a hatchet.

"Pretty good, but I'd rather stick with the machete though," Jeremy replied.

He held up a twenty-two inch, carbon steel blade machete. The blade was jet black and had a rubber grip. Jeremy gave it a twirl and set it down on the counter next to the crowbar he found earlier.

"Not only did I find the hatchet, but I found his big brother too," said Ben.

He held up your standard axe. Wooden handle and a red axe head. It looked like the kind a fireman would carry.

"Do they have ones without wood handles?" Jeremy asked. "The wood ones might break easier. You know?"

Ben nodded, snapped his fingers, and walked down one of the aisles. He returned with a different axe. This one had a yellow handle made out of tough fiberglass. It also had a black axe head, which looked similar to Jeremy's machete blade. Probably made from the same material.

After raiding a knife cabinet and relieving it of some hunting knives, Jeremy noticed that Ben had a concerned look on his face. He still seemed uneasy, despite that they now had some decent weapons.

"What's up man?" Jeremy asked.

Ben turned and looked towards the back of the store.

"Did you notice the door in the back?" He asked.

Jeremy did see the door earlier, but didn't get too close to it, because Ben had already checked that part of the store. He had not thought about it until Ben brought it up.

"Yeah. What about it?"

"Well," Ben started. "It's probably just a storage

area. We haven't checked it out yet. But I could kind smell something bad coming from behind the door."

"We've got weapons now. You wanna check it out?" Jeremy said.

"We probably should. One of those things could be back there."

Jeremy nodded in agreement and grabbed his machete off the counter. Ben picked up his axe and both began to walk towards the door. Jeremy began to feel the adrenaline again. It was not the unsettling feeling of "the rage", but it was better than nothing.

The door was closed, but a light could be seen underneath the door crack. Jeremy looked at Ben before reaching out for the door knob. Ben raised his axe and gave Jeremy the nod to open it.

"One, two, three," Jeremy mouthed, before swinging the door open.

The room was empty except for all the supplies. There was food, soda, more tools and gardening chemicals. They walked in to see that it was a small treasure trove of snack food and carbonated beverages.

"Is this heaven?" Jeremy asked, starting to walk towards a box of candy bars.

Ben grabbed him by the shoulder, holding him back and pointed to the back corner of the room. Slightly hidden behind the mountain of junk food, Jeremy saw two bodies slumped up against the wall. A man and a woman, both wearing matching aprons with the store name on it. Both were holding a pistol and both had a bullet hole directly in the middle of their foreheads.

Chapter Nine

Suicide wasn't something that had even crossed Jeremy's mind at this point. Things were bad, really bad, but kill yourself bad? It seemed way too early to be jumping ship. It had not even been a full twenty-four hours yet. Could the events of the past few hours really be enough reason to off yourself? What made these people think suicide was the answer? Did they see something so terrible that a bullet to the brain seemed like the *easy way out?*

Besides, Jeremy thought to himself. *That would hurt so bad.*

"We should probably grab some food and leave this place, man," Ben said, breaking the silence.

"Why leave? Let's just drag the bodies outside and board this place up," Jeremy said.

"What if the bodies attract those things? Besides, others might get the same idea we had and try to rake this place clean. I'd rather not get into any more human on human confrontations today," Ben answered.

"Yeah, I guess you're right. Touché," Jeremy replied. "So, where we going from here?"

Ben stood there for a moment trying to think of an answer.

"You have any family here? My parents live just out past Rincon. We could go there," he finally said.

"My mom is dead and my dad is off somewhere in the middle of the ocean on his yacht. Sounds like we are going to your place," Jeremy said.

Ben nodded and began to pick up boxes of food.

"Let's grab what we can and get it into the Jeep. I don't think the owners are going to care," he said, motioning towards the bodies.

They both began to grab food and drinks off the

shelves, and carry what they could back to the front door. After accumulating a small pile of snack foods, sodas, and a couple of cases of bottled water, Jeremy walked back to the supply room one last time. He came back carrying the two pistols.

"I don't know how you feel about it, but we should probably take these too. Our tools can only do so much. If we run into any more of those running freaks, it might help to have some kind of firepower, you know?" Jeremy said.

Ben hesitated to take the gun, but nodded as he did. Jeremy was right. Those runners would be too much for hatchets and machetes. He placed it on top of the pile.

"You ready?" He asked Jeremy.

Jeremy nodded and Ben reached to open the door, expecting the worst to be outside. It was clear. Dark, but clear of any dead. It took a few trips to get everything into the back of the Jeep, but as soon as they were done, they pulled away from the store. The guns sat in the center console, ready.

As they drove through Savannah's mid-town, they passed a lot of empty, abandoned cars. Jeremy drove, weaving in and out of the gridlocked mess. Luckily for them, his father really had to have the four wheel drive, despite the fact that he lived in a gated community. Jeremy must have jumped the curb twenty times by now.

"Hey look," Ben said, pointing to their right.

They were passing by the mall. And it was a mess. There were actually people still looting. It looked like Black Friday, maybe worse. The world was going to hell in a hand basket and people were concerned with designer jeans and shoes. The parking lot was not only crowded with living people, but plenty of dead ones too. No doubt all the commotion was attracting them to the mall.

"What kind of idiot would go to the mall at a time like this?" Ben asked.

Jeremy just shook his head and shrugged. Maybe it would have been a good place to hide if it was locked down, but right now, the mall was last on his list of places to go. He watched as one rather large woman fought off a group of zombies with her new Coach purses. She was unsuccessful.

He drove on, trying to put as much distance between them and that madhouse as possible. They rode in silence for a few minutes, both men fighting off exhaustion. What would normally take them a few minutes of driving was taking much longer, due to debris and derelict vehicles. More curb hopping was needed.

"You know what kind of bothers me?" Ben said, breaking the silence.

"What's that?"

"Where exactly is the military in all this? Or any other government official for that matter?"

Ben paused as Jeremy let it sink in. He was right. Jeremy had not thought about it until then, but since he left the store earlier, he had not seen one soldier or police officer. And that just did not make sense.

"I mean, Savannah is surrounded by a military presence," Ben continued. "We have Hunter Army Air Base right here. Fort Stewart just south of us. Parris Island and the Beaufort Air Station right over in South Carolina. We are literally surrounded by the military. But I haven't seen a single soldier, heard a single helicopter or seen any sign that our government is trying to fix this mess in any way. They should be setting up some kind of shelter or refugee camp right?"

"Maybe they are," Jeremy said.

He said it, but he knew it wasn't true. There had been no signs of it. The few minutes that he watched the news earlier, none of it was instructing what to do.

It was all theories of what was happening. It was not reports of what was happening, just media personalities giving their opinions. It wasn't news, it was hearsay.

"Jeremy?" Ben asked, breaking Jeremy's deep thought.

"Sorry," he said. "Just thinking. I know what you mean. I haven't seen anyone either. Except for the one ambulance I saw earlier."

They drove in silence again. Jeremy tried to not think about it too much. The idea of our government backing out on the people was unsettling, not surprising, but unsettling nonetheless. It was weird, but he didn't want to start making conspiracy theories quite yet.

Another car passed them, speeding off in the other direction. The first vehicle to pass them. Jeremy saw people walking as they drove through the city, but cars were scarce. The fact that there were still others alive was a good sign. The city had not been completely overrun by the dead. Yet.

"Which way do you think we should go?" Jeremy asked Ben when they reached DeRenne Avenue.

If they were headed out west towards Rincon, there were really two routes. One would be to get on Veteran's Parkway to I-16. The other would be to cut through downtown and hit up Highway 80 to Highway 21. Either way, it was gonna take a while to get where they were going.

"I don't know, man," Ben said, shaking his head. "It might be a good idea to stay off the parkway. We have no idea how clogged it is. It might be easier to weave in and out through the city streets."

Jeremy nodded and proceeded to press on deeper into the city.

***

"So, what do you do for a living, Ben?"

Ben straightened himself up. Sleep was creeping up on him and was winning the fight. He ran his hand over his face a few times and yawned.

"I, uh, I'm a social media manager," he said.

"Oh, ok," Jeremy replied. "What does that mean?"

Ben laughed.

"Yeah, I get that a lot. Basically, I run all the social media for someone. Facebook, Twitter, Instagram, it's all me. They send me what they want to upload and I make it look good."

"Sounds like something a celebrity would have. Who do you work for around here? There's no celebrities around her- Wait. Are you telling me you work for *Her*?" Jeremy said.

"Ha-ha, yes. Yes, I work for *Her*. The Lady isn't as technologically savvy as she puts off. It's all me. But hey, it's a pretty easy job. I just have to remember to interject *y'all* in there every now and again."

This caused Jeremy to laugh. She did say that. A lot. More than any other southerner should. But hey, Jeremy had no problem with her like some locals did. He would hear some of the older ladies come through his checkout line and complain about her being a sellout and making Savannah look a cartoon. Jeremy always smiled and nodded politely. Sounded like jealous old women to him.

"What about you, Jeremy, what do you do?"

"I *was* a cashier at Publix," he said, remembering Ashley.

"Was... Yeah, I haven't thought about it like that," Ben said. "I guess all I have now is a degree in nothing. Should have learned a trade like my mother suggested."

Jeremy came to a stop when the road ended. He took a left when he got to Victory Drive and it eventually dead ended into Ogeechee Road. He had the choice of going either left or right. To the right, was the Westside of downtown Savannah. They could cut through there and connect with Highway 21, taking them straight to Rincon. Or they could go left and go really out of their way, but stay away from downtown. Jeremy was fixing to turn right, when Ben spoke.

"Hey man, it's really late. And dark. It might be a good idea to wait and tackle the rest of this trip in the morning. It's taken us a while to get where we are now, it might be dawn by the time we make it to my parent's."

"So, what do you want to do?" Jeremy asked.

"I'm exhausted and I'm not even the one driving," he said looking around. "I say we see if one of these warehouses are open and we barricade ourselves in for the night. Just wait it out until morning."

Jeremy looked around. There were a lot of warehouses and industrial looking buildings in the area. Off to the left, he noticed a side road that snaked back in between some of the buildings. He turned down the road. It might be a good idea to find something off the main road a bit.

They passed a few buildings, most of them had gates and fences. All closed.

"Hey look," Ben whispered, pointing to the right.

There was a small, one-story office building with an open yard between it and a warehouse. A chain-link fence with barbed wire closed in the yard between the buildings; a single gate was the only entrance. And it was open. The gate was slightly pushed open, a chain and lock hanging from it. Somebody must have forgotten to lock it up.

Jeremy smiled and nodded. He pulled the Jeep up to the gate and Ben quietly jumped out. He pushed the gate open wide enough for the Jeep to fit through and then once Jeremy was through, closed it back shut. He pulled the chain through the chain-link fence and wrapped it around the posts of the gate. He decided to leave it unlocked, in case they had to bug out in a hurry. Zombies should not be able to get the chain off.

Jeremy parked the Jeep in front of the warehouse and shut the engine off. He stepped out, grabbing the machete and Ben's hatchet. He left the guns in the console. Don't want to make too much noise. The whole area was shrouded in silence.

As they walked up to the door to the warehouse, he handed the hatchet to Ben.

"Better be safe than sorry," he said.

Ben nodded. They both took a deep breath before Jeremy pulled the door open. The lights were on. Somebody must have left in a hurry. The warehouse itself was pretty open. There were stacks of sheet metal and machinery scattered throughout. To the right as they walked in was a picnic table and a small office behind a window. Ben walked over to the window and peered inside.

"What is this place?" Jeremy asked.

"Mock Plumbing and Mechanical," Ben said from the office. "It's some sort of plumbing company."

He was holding up a business card. Jeremy continued to look around, taking in the place where they might be spending the night. A large pile of air duct sat next to one of the large loading doors. That must be what they make here. Duct for air systems and stuff. A large, flat-bed truck with metal gates down the side sat further down at the next loading door.

"Hey, Ben, I think they make other stuff here too. There's a huge pile of air duct over here, so maybe they do more than just plumbing," he said across the warehouse.

No answer.

"Ben?"

Silence. Jeremy turned around to see what was going on. There was Ben with his hands up. And a man.

And a woman. They were both holding guns, the man's shotgun pointed at Ben and the woman's pistol pointed at Jeremy.

"Looks like you boys are gonna have to find some other place to play tickle the pickle," the man said with a crooked grin.

Chapter Ten

"Huh?" Jeremy said.

"You know, tickle the pickle? Hide the salami? Look, however you guys need to express yourself, sexually, well that's your choice," the man asked.

"What does that even mean?" Ben asked, slightly turning to see the man with the gun pointed to his back.

"You guys are gay right? I'm not judging, to each his own..."

"No!" Ben and Jeremy shouted at the same time.

The guy laughed and the woman stepped forward.

"You're going to have to forgive Lexx here, he's... well he's stupid," she said. "You two planning on stayin here? Cause we already had the place scoped out."

"Yeah, dibs," Lexx said.

Jeremy held his hands out in front of him.

"Look, can you at least put the guns down? We're not gonna cause any problems. We're just tired and need a place to rest," he said in the calmest voice he had.

Ben shot him a look that clearly said, 'What the hell are you doing?'

"We don't know what is going on out there," Jeremy continued, ignoring Ben's looks. "We already had enough run-ins with the zombies to-"

"Zombies?" Lexx interrupted. "You think they're zombies? Like in the movies?"

He started laughing uncontrollably, putting his gun down. He bent over holding his stomach.

"This kid thinks they're zombies," he choked out between laughs. "Tori, did you hear him?"

She just shook her head, annoyed with her counterpart, and lowered her weapon. Her glare stayed on Jeremy though. Her bright green eyes cut right into him. The stare might have been worse than the pistol. She stood her ground. Lexx stood back up from laughing, wiping tears away from his eyes.

"Woo. That's rich kid. Whataya? Fifteen? Sixteen?" He asked, still chuckling to himself.

"I'm nineteen," Jeremy said, highly annoyed. "If they're not zombies, then what are they?"

Lexx cocked his head to the side and looked at Jeremy. He just glared at him for a few seconds.

"You gettin' smart with me?" he asked, still looking Jeremy in the eyes.

Jeremy looked over at Ben and then at the woman.

Is this guy for real? He thought.

Lexx walked over to Jeremy, never losing eye contact. He got right in his face. He smelled of cheap cologne. The kind that came out of an aerosol can. It burned the nostrils.

"They are obviously very sick people. Infected with some crazy virus. They ain't zombies kid," he said, very seriously. The man who was all chuckles a moment ago was now as serious as (insert something serious here). He turned and looked at Tori, pointing his thumb at Jeremy.

"Can you believe this kid?" He muttered. "Fuckin' zombies."

"Alright, this has been fun, but I think it's time for you two to leave now," the woman said.

Jeremy took a step closer to them; they both raised their guns in response.

"Whoa. Wait," he started, holding his hands up. "Why can't we both stay here tonight? We can all take turns with keeping watch, that way we all can get some sleep. We're exhausted; I'm sure y'all are too. In the morning, we can go our separate ways. It's a win-win for everybody."

Tori and Lexx both looked at each other. Lexx was shaking his head adamantly no. Tori pursed her lips together and glared at him. He nodded his head and mouthed, 'ok.'

"Deal," she said. "But in the morning, you're gone." Jeremy held his hand out to shake. She grabbed it and gave him the firmest handshake he had ever received.

"You two sure you don't need to get your mommy's permission first before you spend the night," Lexx jeered.

"Hey man," Ben said. "The kid just lost his mom."

Jeremy had tensed up at the statement and not realized it until Ben spoke up. He shook his head, trying to fight back the emotions that were welling up inside of him.

"Hey, sorry kid, I didn't know," Lexx backpedaled. "Like Tori said, I'm dumb."

"It's cool man. You didn't know."

"Listen," Tori interrupted. "We were in the middle of checking the perimeter when we saw you two pull up. It looks like this place is pretty secure. However, we're going to have to figure out some way to secure that front gate," she said. "I don't really want to lock a padlock with no key."

Jeremy looked back to the truck.

"What if we take that truck and park it in front of the gate?" He asked. "That way, we could still get out easily but it would stop them from getting in."

Tori looked at the truck and nodded.

"That should work. Good idea," she said, impressed.

She looked at Lexx and he nodded. He went into the office and found the key box. He grabbed a handful of keys and made his way to the truck. The two of them seemed to have the same "telepathic" communication that Jeremy and Ben shared. Tori turned her attention to Ben.

"So, what's your name?" She asked.

"Ben."

"Well, Ben," she started. "Why don't you go and check all the doors. Make sure they are all secure and locked. If the front one was unlocked, there's a good chance the others might be too."

Ben nodded and walked off. Now it was just Jeremy and Tori. They both stared each other down for a minute; both of them sizing one another up. Jeremy struggled to look her in the eyes. He couldn't help but to notice how beautiful the woman was. Now, then again, he might have been slightly biased since he had been mostly surrounded by dead chicks who have been trying to eat him, but no, Tori was easy on the eyes.

She looked like a runner. Not the dead ones. Her body was tight and slender. She had the potential to kick Jeremy in half. Despite the fact that she had probably been fighting for her life for the past couple hours, she was still well put together. Her scrunchy blonde hair was pulled back into a pony tail. She was wearing a loose-fitting Foo Fighters t-shirt and blue skinny jeans which had a few blood stains on them, but for the most part, she looked clean. Pristine almost.

The truck roared to life across the warehouse. Jeremy snapped out of his daze. Tori walked outside to watch as Lexx parked the truck. Jeremy followed her out. Lexx pulled the truck out in front of the gate and parked it parallel with the fence. He had to climb out the passenger side door due to parking the truck so close to the gate and fence. After climbing under the truck, he closed the gate shut.

"That should do it," he said, walking back towards the building.

The three of them walked back into the building to see Ben standing by the picnic table.

"Hey," he started. "In the back, there's an area that is kinda closed off. Some sort of tool room. We could sleep in there, just in case any of those things get in the warehouse, we'd still have one last line of defense. Also,

I found this foam insulation stuff we can use as beds."

"Good," Tori said. She smiled for the first time.

The four of them made their way back to the tool room. It was walled off by two large sets of shelves. A large iron gate marked "MOCK TOOL ROOM" was the only way in. The four of them walked in and Lexx shut the door behind them. Ben had already taken the foam insulation and torn it into four body length mats.

"It ain't a bed, but it's better than nothing," he said as he passed them out.

Lexx began to move some stuff off one of the shelves, transforming it into a makeshift bunk bed. Tori did the same above him. Jeremy laid his down on a workbench and Ben just put his on the floor.

"Did you see the bathroom too?" Ben asked after placing his mat down.

"Yeah, does it work?" Lexx asked.

"I don't know. I'll go check it out," Ben replied.

He walked out, closing the door behind him.

"Hey, hit some of the lights off too. I got a lantern up on this shelf we could use for light instead," Lexx called out.

"Alright," Ben yelled back.

What was almost a bad situation just a few minutes ago; it now felt that both pairs felt comfortable with each other. Comfortable enough to sleep near each other. The fact that no one was trying to eat each other helped a bit too. When it came down to it, human is human. You'll take what you can get.

Tori jumped down from her shelf, grabbing both Jeremy and Lexx's attention.

"Sorry boys, but I have to do this," she said, reaching her hand up into the back of her shirt. There was a faint click, and then she pulled her arms into her shirt one at a time until she reached up the front, and pulled out her bra. Lexx and Jeremy both just watched, jaws dropped.

"Be free boobies," she said, throwing her bra back on her shelf, rubbing her chest, and then climbing back up to her spot.

"That was the coolest thing I have ever seen," Lexx said.

"Yeah, well wait til I drop a deuce later. You won't think girls are so 'cool' then," she shot back.

"O-M-G. Will you marry me?" Lexx asked.

"Not if you were the last man on earth."

"I wouldn't say that too soon darlin," Lexx said with a chuckle.

The lights went off. Lexx turned his lantern on. The little thing put off some good light, for the most part the tool room was lit. Ben walked back in and lay down on his makeshift bed.

"Did I miss anything?" Ben asked.

"Only the coolest thing ever," Lexx said.

The three of them laughed, Ben sat up and gave them a puzzled look.

"What happened?" He asked.

"Uh, only Tori taking her bra off without taking her shirt off, nothing major," Lexx said. "Tell him how awesome it was Jeremy."

Jeremy didn't say anything for a minute. Tori sat up and looked over at him. He shrugged.

"Ok, it was kinda cool," he admitted.

"Kinda cool? You sure you're not gay, kid? That was freaking amazing," Lexx rambled.

Tori shot Jeremy a quick smile and lay back down.

There was silence for a few minutes. Jeremy tried his best not to think about Tori taking her bra off. He was in plain sight of her and Lexx; he did not need to be pitching a tent where they could see him.

"Anybody else feel like we're at summer camp?" Lexx asked.

"You just don't shut up do you?" Ben asked back.

"No, he doesn't," came Tori's voice from her shelf.

"Well, fine then, why doesn't somebody else talk then? Jeremy how's you end up with Benny boy here?" Lexx huffed.

So, Jeremy told them. He told them about the grocery store. He told them about Ashley and Brian. And how they died. He paused after telling them about his mother. After a minute, he cleared his throat and told them about the Padre. He told them what the Padre said about what was going on. Lexx chuckled to himself up in his "bunk". Jeremy continued and explained how the Padre sacrificed his life so that Jeremy could escape. He explained how much of a douche bag his father was. He ended with the rednecks, the fast zombies, and meeting Ben.

"So, yeah, that's how I got here," Jeremy said.

There was silence for a few minutes as the others soaked in his story.

"Ok. Well I'll go next then," said Ben. He sat up on his bed and began to talk.

Chapter Eleven

"I was visiting my grandmother in the hospital. My adopted grandmother. You see, I'm adopted. My parents are uh... white. So you can imagine the looks I was getting visiting this elderly white woman.

'Why is this young black man coming to see this old white lady?'

Can you believe that? I know we're in the south, but for race to still be such a big issue, it just doesn't make sense. It's 2013 people, c'mon. I guess having our first black president didn't change anything like people hoped, not that I voted for that clown.

Anyways, she was in the hospital recovering from a pretty minor procedure. She didn't come out of it too well, so they put her into a medically induced coma so that she could heal properly. She'd been in there three days so far. Between me and my parents, we always made sure somebody stopped in to check on her.

I had just gotten off work and was stopping by to see her. I replaced her flowers with some new ones I grabbed from the gift shop on my way up. She always loved flowers. She had a garden of her own that she tended to up until her surgery last week. She had me out in that garden so many summers of my childhood. I've been making sure to stop by her house to water her garden too.

I didn't stay long because a nurse came into the room to give my grandmother's roommate a sponge bath. The elderly woman gave me a wink as she began to slip off the top of her hospital gown. I'm gonna be honest, I've seen a lot of scary stuff in the past twenty-four hours, but I'm still gonna put that in the top five."

Everyone chuckled.

"As I was walking out," Ben continued. "I noticed the hospital seemed really busy. I couldn't tell you what 'normal' hospital busy looks like, but it was a lot more busy than when I walked in. Phones were ringing, names were being paged over the intercom, and nurses scurried back and forth all over the place. Hell, looking back on it now, I think I knew something had gone wrong. It's funny how we just refuse to believe that sometimes things go south.

When I finally made it outside, I noticed that the emergency room loading area was slammed with ambulances and cars. Paramedics and doctors were frantically trying to get everyone inside and treated, but there were just too many of them. Doctors began treating patients right there. I heard mothers wailing, husbands shouting, and doctors barking orders. It was complete chaos. My first thought was there had been a terrorist attack.

Can you believe that? It's been over a decade since the towers fell and that's still my first thought. Seems fair enough though, especially with the way our government fumbled over the embassy attack. Anytime some big disaster happens, that thought is there creeping up in the back of our minds. I quickly realized that this was no terrorist attack once I took a good look at the wounded.

The majority of the wounds all seemed very minor. Scratches, cuts, small wounds. It sent shivers down my spine. Why all this fuss for something that some alcohol pads and a bandage could fix? It wasn't adding up. This was something more than some cuts and bruises. I mean, I'm no doctor, but I could tell by the doctor's faces that this was serious situation. Every single one of them had the same look on their face that said, 'This doesn't make sense.' Every single one.

It was then that I saw the first of those things. What are we calling them? Zombies?"

Lexx cleared his throat.

"Sick people," Ben added.

Lexx nodded affirmation.

"At the time I didn't think anything about it, whatever they're called," Ben continued. "It just seemed really strange that in the midst of all this chaos, this one woman stood there in a daze, motionless. Her eyes were dull and grey. Her hair disheveled, like she had just gotten out of bed. She was dressed like it too. A tank top, no bra, and those short shorts that have the writing on the back. You know the ones I'm talking about? The ones that trick you into reading it and then you realize you've been staring at the girl's butt for a minute. If she hadn't been dead, she would have been pretty cute. Is that weird? Can I say that out loud or are you judging me? I'm feeling judged. I didn't know, ok?

She stood there like a statue. Not moving, not even blinking. A nurse finally ran up to her and tried to see if she could dress the wound on her right forearm. It was a small, round mark. It looked like a bite mark. Her eyes followed the nurse's face, still never blinking, just staring. The nurse went to put a bandage on the bite and the girl moaned in response. That was the first time I heard 'the moan.' I don't think I'll ever forget it too. There was a pain and agony in it that shook me to my core.

The nurse tried her best to calm her patient down, but was rewarded with a mouthful of teeth to the face. One bite, two bites, three bites before two doctors tackled her to the ground. It was too late though, as blood poured from the nurse's face. She fell to her knees as she coughed and spurted. Blood was steadily flowing into the hole where her nose had been. The woman was choking to death on her own blood.

She died quickly. The doctors were still struggling with the dead girl, so they didn't see the nurse stand back up. Others began turning too. One man strapped down on a gurney, turned into one of those things, and flipped himself over trying to grab one of the paramedics. The nurse attacked her would-be rescuers, freeing the first girl. Things escalated very quickly.

I don't really remember what happened next. Fear took over and adrenaline surged. I just turned and ran for my car. Like a fucking coward. I wish I could say that I ran back and helped the doctors. I wish I could say that I went back and saved my own grandmother. But I didn't. I just ran. She could be dead, eaten by one of those freaks. Oh God, even worse, she could still be asleep in her room. Can you imagine waking up in the middle of all this? Can you imagine waking up in this world? My brain told me that the hospital would be evacuated, but my heart screamed for me to go back. My legs just didn't listen. They just kept running.

Next thing I knew, I was in the car, driving away from the hospital. I remember tears running down my face. What were my parents going to think? I remember feeling angry with myself. I think that was the first time I felt the- What did you call it, Jeremy? The Rage? Yeah, I felt the rage start to creep up into me. I felt like I was going to rip the steering wheel off. I was sitting at a red light, ready to burst out of my own skin. It didn't last long though as I watched a man run out into traffic and get creamed by a semi.

I didn't know at the time it was one of those crazy runners. It got hit hard and was pulled under the truck. It rolled underneath the truck's tires and crushed both of its legs. It tried to get back up. The rage quickly drained from me and was replaced with pure liquid fear. It crawled a few feet before a car sped by, crushing its head. The head actually got caught in the wheel so that the car dragged its face across the pavement leaving a bright, crimson streak. I blew chunks all over my dashboard.

I ran the red light and shot down Waters. I headed to the nearest gun shop I knew of on Montgomery Crossroads. Not sure why I felt the need to get a gun, but I felt like crap was about to hit the fan. I wanted to be ready for anything.

Well, turns out I picked the wrong gun store. It's where I ran into the aforementioned 'bubbas' who apparently thought too many 'niggers' had guns already. I never even got the chance to look at a gun. The owner didn't want any trouble from them, so he just let them take what they pleased.

I tried to just leave and go on my way, but they wouldn't have it. They shot out the tires on my car, so I took off running. I think they enjoyed 'hunting' me. How sick is that? I hate to think that maybe the dead aren't the ones we will have to worry about. I ran through neighborhoods and jumped over fences like I was in an episode of COPS. I thought I had lost them when I reached Dutch Island, but they cornered me in front of Jeremy's dad's house. And that's when I met up with him."

Ben paused for a minute, thinking to himself.

"I should have gone back for my grandmother. I should have gone back for her. I just left her there. She was in a coma and there was no way for her to protect herself. I don't know if I can ever forget what I did. I don't think I can forgive myself for that."

Chapter Twelve

There was silence as Ben finished his story. Nobody really knew what to say. So, Lexx spoke anyways.

"Hey man, you did what you had to do. Hell, we've all done stuff in the past day that we probably regret. Don't let all these tattoos and my stunning physique fool you. I may look like the bad-boy type, but before yesterday, I wouldn't hurt a fly."

Tori mumbled, "Yeah right."

"I ain't lying babe! Underneath this beautiful exterior is a heart of gold. It's all mutha-fuckin rainbows and southern charm with me," Lexx said with a smile.

"Did you say rainbows?" Jeremy asked. "Cause that sounds kinda gay."

"Not your kind of rainbows fruitcake," Lexx huffed. "Manly fucking-rainbows."

Everybody except Lexx laughed.

"Anyways, as I was saying, I wouldn't hurt nobody. Except Mr. Chan. Oh man, could I hurt that little man. He was always yelling at me. And in some 'ching-chang' language too. I'd be all like, 'Mr. Chan, I can't understand you!' and he'd be all like: 'Ching-chong, ching-chang!'

Yesterday, oh yesterday he pissed me off something good. He was yelling at me, like usual, this time about how I was handling the meat wrong. He kept going on and on about respecting the meat, handling the meat, be gentle with the meat. I could only handle him saying meat so many times. And then he was all was like:

'Lexx, you so ignorant. You so uncultured.'

Ok, so uncultured? Maybe. My parents did name me Lexx with two x's. I wasn't really brought up in a 'cultured' environment. But ignorant? Hells no! Despite my upbringing, I always excelled in school 'n shit. Half the time I was smarter than the teachers! That probably got me in more trouble than anything.

I flipped my lid and told him I quit. He started yelling that I was fire. He meant fired, but kept yelling fire. I was already walking towards the back door when one of the waitresses ran in the kitchen, yelling that one of the customers was choking. So, being the good guy that I am, I ran out into the dining room to see if I could help. When I got out there, the first thing that caught my eye was the pretty little thing on the shelf above me."

"Oh, please," Tori said.

"No, for real babe. The way you were giving that fat guy the Heimlich, kinda turned me on. I was thinking, 'Man, I wish she'd pound me like that.'"

She leaned over the edge of her shelf and shot a dirty look at Lexx.

"I will shoot you," was all she said.

"Yeah, yeah. She was giving the ol' heave-ho to this fat boy who couldn't handle his egg roll. Only thing was, he wasn't choking. He was turning. But we didn't know that at the time. When he had went limp, everyone just assumed he had passed out. But he really died. Tori laid him down and was about to go all mouth-to-mouth on the guy when his eyes shot open.

Everyone was relived at first when he sat back up. We all thought he was fine. That he was ok. That was until he tried to bite 'first responder Barbie' over here.

Man, this girl went from trying to save the guy's life to givin him a knuckle sandwich directly to the face. She sent him sprawling across the floor, but he didn't even seem to register the pain. He scrambled back towards her, jaw flapping up and down as he went. To be honest, I've never seen a guy that big, move that fast!

As soon as he got close enough, Tori gave him a boot to the face and with the skirt she was wearing then, I wouldn't have minded taking a boot to the face either!"

"I didn't get dressed this morning with the idea that I'd be fighting these creeps all the time," Tori said, sighing afterwards. "Luckily I had these jeans in my car. I'd probably just ditched the skirt all together."

"Why did we have to find those damn jeans?" Lexx said with a hint of sadness in his voice, shaking his fist in the air with mock-frustration. "After the boot to the face, fat-boy, as I like to call him, realizes he should pick an easier to acquire snack. He grabs the closest thing to him, which just so happens to be some middle-aged lady. Took a huge chunk out of her arm. Blood started gushing from the wound everywhere.

Now up until that point, everyone had remained relatively calm. I think they were all just in shock, but man, when he bit that lady, the whole place blew up. People started running and screaming. Everybody just panicked. The lady's husband tried to be all hero and ended up being fat-boy's next entrée, if you know what I mean. Not a good scene. Blood everywhere. By this time, Mr. Chan had run back into some backroom. I thought he was a coward and was going to hide. He came back out with one of those ninja swords. Whataya call em? Katanas? Either way, the sword was as big as he was.

He knew how to handle it though. I watched as he scurried over to fat-boy and in one fluid movement, removed the top of the guy's skull from his head. I didn't think the little man had it in him! He really was badass! It seemed so effortless when he did it too. It was almost like he had practiced it or done it before.

Still wasn't enough though. The woman's husband was starting to get back up, which was odd, because she hadn't yet. I tried to warn Mr. Chan, but there wasn't enough time to get the words out. He spun around quickly, only to slice off the guy's arm. It wasn't enough to slow him down, and his six foot, two hundred and fifty pound frame was just too much for Mr. Chan. They both crashed to the floor. The geek got him right in the neck. I heard Mr. Chan scream something Japanese and then watched as his sword thrust straight through both of their skulls."

Lexx paused for a second.

"He knew. I don't know how he knew, but he knew you had to get them in the head. How could he have possibly known that? They weren't lucky guesses. He knew."

He stopped again, lost in thought.

"Yeah, it was strange that he knew that," Tori chimed in. "After Mr. Chan executed both himself and the geek, I gave Lexx a shove towards the back of the restaurant, asking where the back door was. We ran like hell through the kitchen and out into the alleyway. The coast was clear so we took some time to figure out whose vehicle we were going to take. I had a Jeep Cherokee while 'Mr. Tough-Guy' over here drives a hybrid. It wasn't much of a discussion."

"Hey," Lexx interjected. "We probably wouldn't have run out of gas like we did!"

"Yeah," she continued on. "We also wouldn't have been able to go off road like we needed to. And boy did we have to go off road! The only thing worse than Savannah rush hour traffic is Savannah rush hour traffic during the end of the world. These people do not know how to drive!"

Ben chimed in, "So, what were you doing at the restaurant Tori?"

"I was waiting on a blind date who I'm pretty sure stood me up. No big deal though. The guy had a horse face," she said matter-of-factly.

"I must say that you are one of the most straight forward women I have ever met," Ben added.

"Yeah, I get that a lot," she replied. "My father was-is a Marine. He's stationed out at Parris Island. I'm the son he never had. When my mom passed away, I was the only woman in his life. He did his best with me, but I'm a little rough around the edges because of it. Growing up around Marines will have that effect on you. I'm no tomboy mind you, I like to dress up, and go out drinking downtown with the girls too. It's just not the end of the world when I break a nail, you know?"

She yawned. This started a chain reaction of yawning.

"Look," she said. "We all need to get some sleep if we're going to be any good tomorrow. I'll take first watch and I'll wake you up in a few hours, okay Ben? Then you can wake up Jeremy and Lexx can take last watch."

"Sounds good," Ben yawned.

Lexx passed the lantern up to Tori and she dimmed the light so that it was barely on. Jeremy lay there in the darkness; his mind racing with the day's events. He glanced up at Tori, who was propped up in her "bunk", scanning the warehouse for anything suspicious. She noticed his staring, which he quickly redirected his gaze. He could have sworn he saw her smile.

"This really doesn't feel like camp to anyone else?" Lexx asked. "I'm just sayin'. This feels a lot like camp."

Ben started laughing, but it wasn't long before everyone else joined in. Even Tori.

"Sure, man. This does feel like camp," Ben said, his laughter trailing off. "And just like camp, let's get some sleep."

"Okay. I'm gonna rock that zip line tomorrow though," Lexx said, letting out a big yawn.

It was answered by more yawns. Jeremy felt his eyes grow heavy. His mat wasn't the most comfortable bedding in the world, but right now, it was heaven. As he fell asleep, he tried his best not to think of Tori taking her bra off.

***

Earlier, when Tori and Lexx were checking the perimeter of the yard, they searched carefully for any kind of weak point. The warehouse ran along one side of the yard and the office building ran along three quarters of the other side. A chain-link fence topped in barbed wire ran across the front and back sides.

The back of the yard was covered by metal roofing and filled with all kinds of plumbing fittings and material. PVC and cast iron pipe, elbows and tee's littered the ground. They were inspecting several bins of fittings when Ben and Jeremy pulled up, leaving the bins to go see who was entering the gate.

If they had only gone back a little further, they would have found a shelving unit full of more material. But it wasn't the shelves that they needed to see. Hidden behind the shelves was a drainage ditch that ran parallel with the back fence. The running of water over the years had created a small gulch underneath the fence. Jagged rocks would have made it difficult to access, but to someone not worried about pain, they would serve as no deterrent.

Chapter Thirteen

Jeremy's eyes shot open. He lifted his head off of the table and looked around. He was in the break room at work. He must have dozed off. His empty energy drink can sat in front of him.

Was it all a dream? He thought. *Did I just dream all of that?*

He looked at the clock. It was only 4:15. He'd been asleep for five minutes. It had all been a dream. A really fucked-up dream. It was cliché, but he pinched himself to make sure. Yes. Pain. He sighed a breath of relief and went to stand up, but as he did, Ashley walked into the room.

"Jeremy, what are you doing? Brian is looking for you!"

He went to open his mouth, but she placed her finger on his lips and pushed him back down on his chair. She quickly straddled him and sat on his lap.

"I've been looking for you," she whispered seductively into his ear.

She slowly ran her hands through his hair, tugging his head back gently, but firmly, as she began to kiss on his neck.

What is going on? He thought; his mind racing.

And then it became evidently clear as another figure entered the room. This woman was slender, like a runner. Her blonde hair was long and full of tight curls. It hung loose around her head, but would look equally good pulled into a pony tail. She was wearing a loose-fitting Foo Fighters t-shirt, with one shoulder exposing a bright red bra strap. She was wearing no pants; her smooth legs tight and muscular like someone who ran.

Oh no, Jeremy thought.

The woman walked over to him, as Ashley

continued to nibble on his neck. She reached up into her shirt and unclasped her bra.

Oh no, oh no.

He was dreaming. This wasn't happening. He tried to shake himself awake, but the two of them held him down.

"You want to leave us?" Ashley asked painfully.

"You're not real!" Jeremy yelled. "This is a dream!"

He squirmed to get free, but the two women's grip was solid.

"Oh, Jeremy. Don't you think we're pretty?" Ashley asked, as the skin from her face began to fall away.

It fell in clumps to the floor, until finally just muscle and bone was exposed.

Wake up Jeremy! WAKE UP!

***

Jeremy's eyes shot open. He awakened to Lexx looming over him, one finger pressed up to his lips. The man had a very serious look on his face. He took the finger from his lips and pointed towards outside.

Jeremy nodded. Something was wrong.

Tori and Ben were both already awake. Tori was checking her weapon. Ben was at the cracked back door peering out. She moved over next to him, pushing him aside. She shook her head and closed the door. Jeremy stood up and moved towards the others. He could feel tension in the air.

"How the hell did that thing get in here?" Tori whispered harshly. "You were supposed to be keeping watch Lexx!"

"Me? You had first watch!" He shot back.

She swore under her breath.

"Let's just go shoot it and be done with it," Ben interjected.

"And attract more of them with a gunshot or its

moan? I don't think so," Tori said.
Silence.
"So, what do we do?" Jeremy finally spoke.
"We take it out. Quietly," Tori said.

They began collecting their weapons. Ben grabbed his hatchet; Jeremy his machete. Tori grabbed a crowbar from the tools borrowed from the hardware store. Lexx ran out of the back room and returned quickly with an odd looking hammer. It had a square head, flat sides, and a long, chisel-like end.

"Found this up on one of the work tables. Should do the trick," he said with a smile.

"Alright," Tori started. "Who wants to be the bait?"

"Bait?" Ben asked.

"Yeah, someone is going to have to distract it while the rest of us run up behind it and bash its brains in."

"I'll do it," Jeremy said, not waiting for someone else to volunteer. He shocked himself with the willingness he just had. He'd never do that at work.

Tori nodded. She motioned for Jeremy to move towards the door.

"We'll wait for you to get its undivided attention, then we'll flank it and take it out. Sound good?"

Jeremy nodded and stepped outside.

As good as it's gonna get.

***

The zombie wandered around the yard aimlessly. He was a large one too. Easily over three hundred pounds. Jeremy could not tell if it was always this big or was bloated from "over-eating." Whoever he was before he died, he did not mess around when it came to getting food.

Let's hope that's changed, Jeremy thought to himself. *Who am I kidding? Look at this fat fucker.*

Jeremy slowly crept around the large oak tree that

seemed to grow out of the center of the yard. The fat boy, as Lexx would say, was on the other side of the tree, standing there in a daze. It just stood there. A twitch or leftover muscle spasm every now and then, but other than that it was glued to the spot it stood on. As Jeremy was about to come around the tree into view, the zombie started sniffing the air. Maybe sniffing is not the correct word. Snorting? Inhaling large amounts of air through the bulbous piece of flesh that used to be its nose? Either way it smelled something. It smelled food. It smelled Jeremy.

"Hi there," Jeremy said, as he walked out from behind the tree. "Do you have a minute to talk about the Lord Jesus?"

The zombie snapped out of its daze and lunged for Jeremy.

"You know, for a big fella, you got some speed in you! What's wrong? Don't like fast food? Cause I couldn't tell!"

It did not seem fazed by Jeremy's sarcastic taunts. It wanted to kill him anyways. Jeremy ran towards the gate where they parked the truck the night before. The geek shambled after him as fast as its short, stubby little legs could carry it. Jeremy stopped and waited for the thing to catch up. The three others were sneaking up behind it. It was so focused on Jeremy that it didn't even notice.

"C'mon big boy! Come and get me," Jeremy shouted at it.

Its jaw was clamping up and down, drool dripping down its decaying chin. Ben ran up behind him, and raised up his axe, prepping to bring it down on the zombie's head. He lost his footing, tripped, and brought down the axe on the freak's shoulder instead of the death dealing head blow he planned. Its arm went flying, the axe cleaving straight through the soft, rotted flesh. The axe head kept going and clipped the side of the zombie's massive stomach. Blood, puss, and bile spewed from the hole.

It finally turned to its attackers and seeing Ben on the ground, reached out for him first. It did not even seem fazed that it was missing an arm and juices were shooting out of its side like a geyser. Ben scrambled backwards, kicking at the ghoul. Lexx ran up and brought the chisel end of his hammer down on the z's head. It seized, then went limp, and collapsed into a heap in front of Ben. A large, brown puddle of blood and feces collected around the mountain of dead flesh.

"Well, that was easy," Lexx said, trying to catch his breath.

He did not even get the words out of his mouth before one of the crazies began shrieking off in the distance. Others joined in and moans began to fill the air. They all looked towards the fence. Zombies were coming from everywhere. The fence was now lined with walking corpses. The crazies arrived and began climbing over the fences. They hit the barbed wire and did not stop as it ripped chunks of flesh and meat from their bones. Their bright, red blood showered all over their slower comrades.

"Run!" Tori yelled.

They all booked it for the back door to the warehouse. Jeremy broke out into a full out sprint. He looked over his shoulder and saw that two of the crazies had untangled themselves from the barbed wire and were running after the survivors.

They're mangled but yet still so fast, he thought.

Jeremy was a pretty decent runner. He ran cross country in high school, the one extracurricular activity he did besides work. But you don't get scholarships for being responsible and holding down a part time job in high school. So, cross country it was then. But that was in high school and once he graduated he didn't run as much as he used to. No time when you're trying to help your mom make ends meet.

Right now though, he summoned up whatever leftover speed he had, and ran like a madman towards the door. The others had been a little closer, but he passed both Ben and Lexx on the way there. Tori held the door open and was shouting for them to get inside. Jeremy ran inside and was followed by Lexx. As Ben entered, one of the crazies reached the door and grabbed him by the shirt. Jeremy quickly brought his machete down on its arm. It fell back and down the stairs, Lexx slamming the door shut.

"Oh shit, oh shit, oh shit," Ben muttered over and over.

"Get yourself together!" Tori barked. "We've got to get up to the front of the building. They saw us come in the back, so they'll be back here trying to get in. Let's go."

They ran towards the front of the warehouse. Lexx grabbed Tori's bra on the way.

"Hey, you might want this!" He said with a boyish smile.

"You keep it!"

"Yes! Merry Christmas to me!"

He held it up to his nose as they made their way up front. When they got there, Tori went up to the door and pushed her ear against it. She was listening to see if it sounded like any zombies were right outside the door. She held her head there for a few seconds but it felt like hours.

"Sounds clear."

"Oh, man... What about the truck?" Jeremy asked, just realizing that the twenty foot flatbed truck that they had parked in front of the gate the night before to *protect* them from an attack was now trapping them inside during an attack. Not a good situation.

"Shit. That's right. How are we gonna move that truck?" Tori said.

A brief silence.

"I got this," Lexx said, with an unwavering assurance.

Tori started to protest, but Lexx, in all his macho bravado, put a finger up to her lips and shushed her.

"I got this."

He stretched out his hands in front of him and cracked his knuckles. He walked up to the door, but then turned back to the others.

"Look, I'm going to go out there and move the truck. As soon as you hear the engine crank, you run to the Jeep and get the fuck out of here. No matter what happens to me, you get outta here. You understand?"

The three of them nodded.

"Alright then, here we go," he said.

He reached for the door knob.

"Wait!"

Tori walked up to him and planted a kiss on his cheek.

"Be safe you idiot," she said.

He smiled.

"Of course."

With that he opened the door and ran out towards the truck.

***

Lexx ran full sprint towards the gate. Tori was right. All the zombies, the crazy ones, had made their way back towards the back door. They didn't even notice Lexx yet. The slower, dumber ones along the fence on the other hand, they noticed. They pushed against the fence. It swayed against the weight of the dead.

When he reached the gate, he yanked the unlocked chain through. The noise grabbed the attention of the crazies. He cursed himself under his breath. They shrieked in response to the clanging of metal chain

against the metal chain-link fence. Lexx swung the gates open and quickly climbed into the truck. He left the keys in the ignition, just in case something did happen, and they had to get out quick. He promptly turned the keys, the diesel engine roaring to life. Being quiet was really no longer an issue. He threw it into reverse and began to back the truck over the line of walking dead behind him. The sound of bones cracking and the jostling of the truck brought a faint smile to Lexx's face.
Fuck 'em.

***

"There's the engine! Let's go!" Tori yelled.
The three of them bolted out into the sunlight, a stark contrast from the darkness inside of the warehouse. As their eyes adjusted, they scrambled for the Jeep. Jeremy ran towards the driver's seat with keys in hand. He jumped in, then Tori, and then Ben. As Ben was climbing in, Jeremy turned the keys in the ignition and the Jeep came to life. He floored it in reverse, taking out one of the crazies in the process. He threw it into drive and sped out the gate. They saw Lexx and the truck still reversing over the dead down the street.
"We'll wait for him around the corner," Jeremy said, seeing the concern wash over Tori's face.
She nodded, her eyes fixed on the large truck behind them. Jeremy sped around the curves and pulled back out onto Highway 17. He pulled the Jeep over right before a bridge that went over train tracks. Shifting into park, he turned and joined Ben and Tori in looking out the back of the Jeep. His mouth slowly dropped as he watched the truck cross the highway in flames, followed by dead corpses also on fire, and crash into another warehouse.

Chapter Fourteen

The flames from the warehouse burned brightly in the afternoon sun. Thick, black smoke rose up slowly into the clear blue sky. The three of them stared on in shock. Lexx was dead. He crashed the truck into the warehouse so they could escape. Someone else had given their life so that Jeremy could live. Someone again who barely knew him. Jeremy was the first to snap out of it.

"We have to go."

"We have to go see if he made it," Tori protested.

Jeremy looked into her eyes. He could see that she was fighting back tears. Although they said they only met yesterday, Jeremy felt that the two were closer then they let on. Surviving with someone will have that effect on you. Jeremy felt a companionship between Ben and himself. He gently placed his hand on her shoulder.

"He didn't make it. There's no way someone could survive that..."

She sat there in silence. She had grown somewhat attached to Lexx. They had been together since the outbreak in the restaurant, and as goofy as he was, she knew she could trust him. He couldn't be gone. It's crazy how when the world falls apart how quickly trust can be built or broken.

"Ok," she finally said. "Let's go. He wouldn't want us to waste his sacrifice."

Jeremy put the Jeep back into drive and turned the Jeep around. He stopped for a moment, staring at the wreckage, and the burning building.

"Where are you going?" Ben asked from the back seat.

"We'll cut through the edge of downtown and get on I-16 from there."

Ben nodded. Tori slunk down in her seat and staring out the passenger window; her eyes glazed over lost in thought.

"Where are you guys going?"

Jeremy and Tori spun around as Lexx climbed into the backseat.

"Lexx!" The three of them shouted in unison.

"Yeah?" He asked, grinning.

"We thought you were dead, man!" Ben said.

"How did you? Where did you?" Jeremy stammered in sheer surprise.

Lexx just grinned, his smile from ear to ear.

"What? Did you think I was still in the truck? Haha, that's rich! I lit a rag on fire and stuffed it into the fuel tank, threw that bad boy in drive, and dropped a box of screws on the gas pedal. Got the truck rollin' in the right direction and ditched it. The geeks didn't even notice me drop out. They were too preoccupied with the burning truck. Those dumb ass-bags even caught themselves on fire!"

Tori's countenance changed, she was now trying to hide her happiness behind a smirk of disapproval.

"What's wrong, babe? Did you miss me?" Lexx asked, leaning in towards Tori's direction.

"I'd be lying if I didn't say yes. Don't get too excited about it," she replied.

"I told ya you'd find me irresistible," he said with a boyish smirk.

"Well, don't plan on getting down on one knee quite yet. I still don't *like* you."

"I can live with that," he said, leaning back in his seat. "I only regret that I left your bra in the truck."

"Oh, I'm *sure* that was an accident," she said.

Lexx chuckled.

"Maybe. Maybe not. We'll never know for sure. Now Jeremy, if you would be so kind, would you kindly get us the fuck out of here?"

"With pleasure," Jeremy answered, as he floored it towards downtown Savannah.

***

The neighborhood they passed through was rough looking. And that was before this whole zombie thing broke out. Savannah was weird like that. She had this beautiful historic downtown, coastal marsh land, and beautiful architecture, but at the same time, she had her fair share of projects, trailer parks, and ghettos. As some parts of the city moved forward in progress, other parts were left behind to rot, no matter how much the Savannah College of Arts and Design tried to restore them to former glories. The diversity of Savannah is spread wide. From SCAD students to the homeless, from old money to no money, Savannah was dripping with culture.

Jeremy was unsure of what culture was dripping from the doorways of the houses they were passing. It seems that the hood ain't no different from the islands when it comes to the dead coming back to life. Zombies don't care how much you make, or your skin color, they just want to eat you.

He made a left turn when he came to the end of the street. Another fork in the road. Left would take them around the outskirts of downtown a bit more. Right would have taken them to MLK Jr. Boulevard, aka the edge of downtown. Jeremy wanted to stay out of downtown as much as possible. Too many corners and tight streets to navigate. Too dangerous. Even in the Jeep, the last thing they needed was to get stuck on one of Savannah's squares surrounded by the dead.

As Jeremy bobbed and weaved through abandoned vehicles, he noticed the cemetery to the left of them. One of Savannah's countless historic cemeteries. Graves for as far as the eyes could see, until old oak trees blocked your view. The trees have probably been there longer than some of the graves themselves. The tombstones looked weathered by time, fading in the sunlight. They looked peaceful.

It was then that Jeremy realized something about the cemetery.

"Hey guys," he said out loud.

"Yeah?" Lexx asked, the other two perking up as well.

"Check out the cemetery," Jeremy said, pointing with one hand.

The three others looked out towards where Jeremy had pointed. They stared for a moment before Lexx looked back at Jeremy.

"Yeah? What about it?" He asked with a puzzled look on his face.

"There's no dead rising."

They all looked back over towards the cemetery. Jeremy was right. No graves looked disturbed. There was no dead coming out of the ground like you see in the movies. No hands trying to break free from the earth. Just rows and rows of tombstones and crypts like you would normally see.

"What does that mean?" Tori asked.

"I guess," Jeremy started, "I guess it means that whatever this is going on, it doesn't affect the already deceased. It only affects the living."

They all rode in silence as they let Jeremy's words sink in. It wasn't necessarily good news, but it at least meant that this sickness only affected the living inhabitants of the planet. All seven billion of them. He continued to snake his way through towards West Bay Street. They were passing under I-16 at the moment. Sleeping bags and trash could still be seen under the overpass.

"What if they just haven't gotten out yet?" Ben asked, finally speaking.

"What do you mean?" Jeremy said.

"Well," Ben said, "What if they just haven't dug their way up yet? Bodies are buried six feet under, right? Maybe they haven't made it up all the way yet. It hasn't even been a full twenty four hours yet. I don't know, just thinking out loud."

"I don't think we will have to worry about them then. They'll starve themselves out before they break through the casket and six feet of packed in dirt," Jeremy responded.

Ben nodded, Jeremy's answer seemed sufficient for him. He went back to daydreaming out the window.

"Hey, Jeremy, can you stop the Jeep for a moment?" Tori asked.

Everyone looked at her as Jeremy slowed the Jeep to a stop. She looked like she was thinking about something.

"Um, well, my dad is a drill instructor out on Parris Island and I know the plan is to head west, but if we can make it there, maybe it's safe. Maybe Parris Island is okay? Plus, it would be great to know if he's okay too. I mean, I know he is, it would just be nice to see him."

Jeremy looked at Ben and he had the same look of concern.

"Look, Tori," Jeremy said. "I'm sure your dad is fine, but when me and Ben drove by Hunter, it seemed vacant. And-"

"Well, yeah," she interrupted. "That's the Army. Of course they'd be overrun. My dad's a *Marine*. Marines don't get overrun."

Lexx laughed. Ben looked back at Jeremy and shrugged.

"You think he'll still be there?" Jeremy asked.

"I know he will. He'll be expecting me to make my way to him. That was our plan anyways," she said, motioning towards Lexx.

"Ok, then. South Carolina it is then. Any

objections?"

Lexx shook his head and smiled. Ben, on the other hand, looked concerned.

"*Our* plan was to head west. Out past Rincon. My parents live out there," he said.

Tori turned in her seat to face Ben.

"Do you think they're still alive?" she asked.

Ben nodded, albeit slowly.

"Well, if we get to Parris Island, we can better supply you to go find them. The base is going to be our best shot for survival, Ben," she said softly.

Everyone in that Jeep knew that if they could make it to the Marines stationed there, they just might survive this thing. Ben nodded again. He knew she was right; he just didn't like the idea of leaving his parents alone out there much longer.

They were stopped in front of one of SCAD's many student housing units, a clear view of the Talmadge Bridge in front of them. Once they got over the suspension bridge, it would be an hour drive to Parris Island. Granted they didn't run into any hang-ups. Or dead. Traffic seemed to be moving over the bridge. Slowly, but moving.

Ben leaned in towards the front of the Jeep.

"Do y'all hear that?"

Everyone else got quiet and Jeremy lowered the windows. It was the low rumble of fighter jets in the distance. They watched as a pair of jets did a flyby of the bridge, passing just over the top of it. The two jets were flying much lower than usual.

"What are they doing?" Ben asked.

"Probably just some surveillance. Those are Marine fighters, probably from the Air Station in Beau-"

The two jets made abrupt turns and raced towards the bridge at breakneck speeds. As they got closer, you could see each jet drop something that raced off in the direction of the bridge. Both planes took off into the sky, disappearing into the clouds and sunlight.

The bridge exploded in a huge blast of fire and debris.

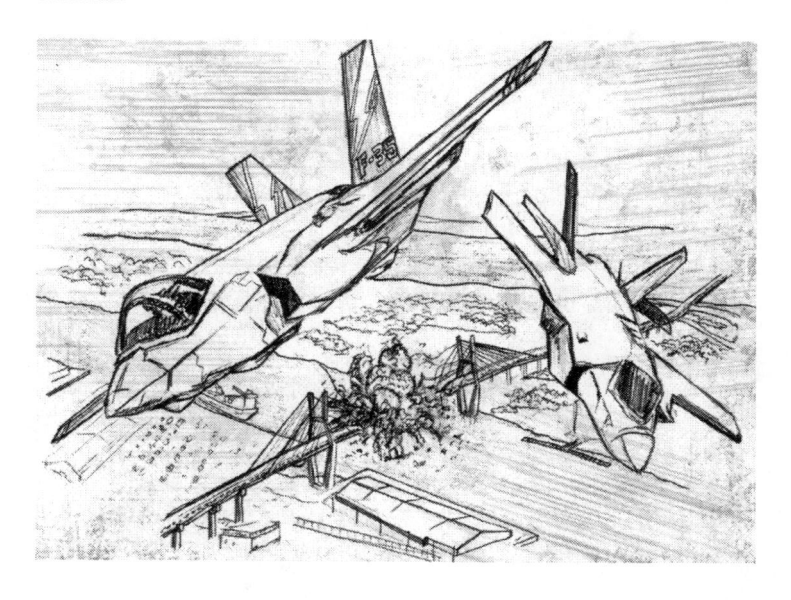

Chapter Fifteen

"What the hell?" Lexx yelled over the shockwaves and roar of the explosion, as they watched in shock as the bridge collapsed, and cars began to tumble into the Savannah River.

They could see the panic erupting on both side of the bridge. The cars that survived the blast were trying to push each other out of the way, trying to get away from the flames and heat. They pushed into each other, failing at breaking free, and only making the situation worse. Full panic had set in.

"How could they just bomb the bridge?" Lexx continued to yell, not giving a damn who heard him.

"There were people on that bridge! Tori, you said those were *Marine jets*?"

She nodded slowly as she continued to stare at the remaining pieces of bridge. Her mouth was wide open in shock. A single tear ran from her eye down her cheek.

How could they? She thought. *How could they?*

Lexx was no longer yelling things, just swearing under his breath over and over. Ben too was in shock, not moving with his eyes closed. If he could just shut his eyes and maybe the bridge will still be there.

Maybe it didn't happen. The military wouldn't do that. Not our military. Would they? He thought.

The thoughts raced through Jeremy's mind as well, but they quickly got pushed aside as his survival instinct kicked in. They had to abandon going to Parris Island. If the Marines were going to bomb the Talmadge Bridge, then they most likely would not take too kindly to visitors. The government must be trying to contain the spread of infection. That had to be it. And the fact that they were willing to take these kind of measures, well, that meant things just got pretty damn serious.

"We can't go to Parris Island now."

"And why not Jeremy?" Tori asked, snapping out of her daze and seeming agitated by his statement.

"Well," he started. "For starters, the bridge we needed to cross just got blown up. Secondly, we're pretty sure the place we were headed to are the same guys who blew it up. I'm sure your dad is a nice guy Tori, but I don't think his friends will be as welcoming."

"Those must have been rogue pilots. There's no way the United States Marine Corps is going to bomb a bridge with fucking civilians on it!" she yelled.

"Either way, Tori," Jeremy continued, calmly. "We physically cannot get there. The only other way is to get to I-95 and cross over into South Carolina that way, but I think it might be safe to assume that they'll take out that bridge too. Unless you have a boat? Do you have a boat? No? Ok, then. Look, I think the government is trying to stop the infection of whatever this is from spreading. They're taking some pretty serious measures, so things must be going really bad all over. Not just here."

She huffed for a second, mulling over what he was saying.

"What about the bridge near Port Wentworth? It's a smaller bridge and maybe-"

"I'm sure they'll take that one out too Tori," Jeremy interrupted, gently.

"So what do we do then? What's the plan now Jeremy?"

She shot him a stare that questioned his position of authority. A position he just put himself into unintentionally. Lexx and Ben also both looked at Jeremy for an answer as well.

"Yeah, man," Lexx said. "What's the plan?"

Jeremy thought for a second. His mind raced as he played out possible scenarios and decisions.

"We go back to the plan from before. We head west. Ben's parent's live outside of Rincon, right Ben?"

Ben nodded.

"Okay, for now we head there, but we need to get away from Savannah as soon as possible. The city is heavily populated and will most like be concentrated with dead soon. We need to get out into the country. Less people, less zombies."

They took a minute to discuss the plan. Tori wasn't ready to give up on finding her dad, but also had no idea on how to get to him. South Carolina might as well be the other side of the world now. Ben wanted to find his parents. He was confident they would be at the house. He made his case that they would have plenty of food and supplies. His parents even had an RV they could probably use.

Lexx stayed quiet mostly. As the other three bickered about what they were going to do, he kept watch on what was going on outside the Jeep. The explosion had attracted the attention of a lot of zombies. They were coming out from all over the place. The ruckus from inside the Jeep was probably not the best idea either.

"Hey guys, I hate to break up this lovely conversation you have going on here, but I think it's time for us to get goin," he said, motioning towards outside.

A good sized group of z's had gathered around the Jeep. While most were focused on the flames near the bridge, some were starting to take notice of the Jeep and what was inside the Jeep. One let out a moan which was answered by another. And another. And another.

Jeremy put the Jeep back in drive and slowly started creeping forward. The dead began to shamble in the direction of the moving vehicle. He picked up speed, trying to dodge the maze of derelict vehicles, and outrun the pursuing dead. They were slow, but he could only go so fast through the abandoned streets.

"Uh, they are gaining on us," Ben said. He was fixed on the rear window.

Jeremy sped up, scraping the side of an old hatchback with mismatched hubcaps.

"Easy, Jeremy!" Tori yelled from the passenger seat.

"I'm trying!"

Ben continued to keep his eyes peeled on the back window. He scanned the amassing crowd of dead. There just kept being more of them. It was as if the whole city was behind them. There was no way there could be this many dead already. Maybe it was a good idea to bomb the bridge.

"Where do I go?" Jeremy asked frantically, as he came up to MLK.

"Take a right and then a left on Anderson," Tori answered.

He jerked the wheel to the right and hopped the curb onto MLK Jr. Boulevard. Anderson was two blocks down, past Henry. Both were one way streets, each one heading the opposite way. He made a hard left onto Anderson when he got there, not bothering to wait for the still functioning stoplight.

"Oh, shit," Ben started cursing from the backseat.

"What is it?" Jeremy and Tori both yelled at the same time.

"We got runners."

Behind them, breaking through the crowd of slower zombies was a handful of runners. They pushed and pulled their dead comrades out of the way. Their bright, red blood and still pink skin was at a stark contrast to the sea of grey, rotting, dead flesh surrounding them.

"Must go faster!" Ben yelled.

Jeremy floored it. Anderson was surprisingly clear

of traffic. A random zombie here and there, but very few cars. The freaks behind them started shrieking. One flew through the air, launching itself off another zombie and in front of the pack. Others followed and they all broke out into full sprint. One of them, what was once a young woman, must have landed wrong because she fell, and rolled like a rag doll. She tried to get back up but the bone was visibly broken in her right leg. It pierced through the skin right above the ankle.

The freaks were picking up speed and gaining on the Jeep. Jeremy stomped down the pedal as he raced down Anderson.

"Does anybody else feel like we're in that one scene from Jurassic Park?" Lexx asked.

"Shut up Lexx!" Tori answered.

"Where to now?" Jeremy yelled, swerving away from a smoldering sedan.

"Turn left onto Bull, no, left on Drayton!" Tori yelled back. "I have an idea."

"Oh, that's not good," Lexx laughed.

She shot him a look that told him to shut up. He shrugged and smiled. Ben yelled up a report on the crazies. There were three of them and they were about two car lengths behind. He began thinking out loud as to why they were so fast. He muttered something about them not registering pain and therefore not dealing with muscle fatigue.

Jeremy saw the sign for Drayton and steered hard left onto the street. Another one way street. The slower dead were way back now, most losing interest, but the runners were still there.

"Okay, what's the plan Tori?" He said in a condescending manner, getting her back from earlier.

"Does this thing have four wheel drive?"

"Uh, it's a Jeep isn't it?"

"Cut through the park."

"What?!" All three men said at once.

"Cut through the park and bob through the trees. Right now we're on flat ground and they're gaining on us. If we cut through the park we might lose them," she said, her voice much calmer.

"I don't know if that's a good id-"

Ben was unable to finish his sentence before Jeremy jerked the wheel to the left, jumped the curb, and roared across the grass of Forsyth Park.

Chapter Sixteen

Grass and dirt shot out from behind the Jeep as it raced across the open field. Jeremy steered towards the large oak trees in the middle of the park. There was a wide enough walkway there between the rows of trees that the Jeep would easily fit on. Once they reached the walkway, Jeremy turned right, facing downtown. The runners were still close behind them, maybe two car lengths. They didn't seem tired. Didn't seem fazed at all.

Passing a large statue, with what looked like a confederate soldier on it, the Jeep sped by benches that once held the butts of tourists and locals alike. The park was split into basically two parts. The southern "half" was made of two large, open fields where locals and out-of-towners would come for picnics, to play flag football, or even a rowdy game of ultimate Frisbee. The northern "half" on the other hand was made up of southern staple plant life, such as Live Oaks, Magnolias, and Azaleas. The scent of Jasmine permeated through the air. A large fountain sat in the middle of the northern garden. It was often the background for postcards, Instagram shots, and bridal pictures. While Savannah was going to hell in a hand basket, this park seemed to still hold on to its majesty somehow. Even the water in the fountain was still running.

Jeremy reached the canopy of the trees and began to bob and weave through them as Tori had suggested. The dead were having trouble keeping up. He frantically zigzagged through. Lexx let out a holler of excitement. He had a smile on his face like a little boy on a roller coaster. Ben looked sick.

"Oh! Oh! Oh! Look! Look!" Lexx yelled from the backseat. "Zombie wedding! Zombie wedding!"

The three others looked out to the right of the Jeep and standing near the fountain was what looked like the remaining bits of a bridal party. The bride wore white. Stained with blood, but still mostly white. Her groom stood next to her dressed in a tattered black tux. They were still holding hands. The rest of the bridal party was there too. The saddest of which were the bridesmaids. They had died in really ugly dresses and would remain that way forever.

"Holy shit," Tori said.

"I know right?" Lexx replied. "How do you think that happened? Wouldn't be great if the Priest turned and attacked them? Oh, oh, what about the mother of the bride? Oh yeah, that had to be it..."

The wedding party noticed the Jeep, but also noticed how fast it was moving. They did not pursue. To be fair, it seemed that they were in the middle of taking pictures and that it something you *do not* want to mess with. Jeremy kept going through the trees, the runners now falling way behind.

"Are they still behind us?" Jeremy yelled to the backseat.

"Uh... no. Wait, there's one still pretty close," Ben answered sickly.

"How close?"

"Twenty feet, maybe?"

Jeremy spun the Jeep around to a stop. The runner came out from behind a tree and ran full speed towards them, letting out an angry shriek. In a small bit of irony, the zombie was wearing running shorts and a marathon t-shirt. He was literally a runner. Looking to be in pretty good shape too, if it wasn't for the bright red blood dripping from his mouth, and the missing right-forearm, you'd think this guy was just going for a run through the park. His eyes were bloodshot. Probably would explain why he did not see what came next.

Jeremy floored it and made a beeline for the runner. The runner didn't slow down. Jeremy didn't slow down. Jeremy kept his eyes on the zombies until the very last moment. Never once did he see that look that every human gets when they realize they played chicken with the wrong person.

The Jeep and corpse collided, sending the body tumbling below the Jeep's tires. Jeremy didn't stop, but turned the Jeep towards the street.

"Holy shit, Jeremy! What the fuck?" Tori yelled.

It didn't seem to faze him. He pulled the Jeep out onto Whitaker Street and headed deeper into downtown. Whitaker was another of the many one way streets in Savannah. Jeremy was going the wrong way. But road rules were the last of his concern. They'd lost their tail of runner zombies, but many of the "regular" ones were still all over the place. Most reached out for the speeding Jeep, but that was about as much effort they put forward.

"Jeremy, would you like to explain what the hell that was back there?" Tori asked.

"I don't know," he shrugged. "Seemed like a good idea at the time."

"Are you fu-"

"We need to get out of the city," he interrupted. "We may have lost the runners, but this place is infested with dead."

"Well, that was the plan wasn't it?" Tori said, exasperated.

He nodded ignoring her tone.

"Cut him some slack, Tori," Ben said from the backseat.

She turned around and shot him a dirty look.

"It was a stupid move and it could have cost us the Jeep. That corpse could have just as easily rolled onto the hood, cracked the windshield, and showered us with infected goo. Do you want that? I bet he didn't think about that."

Ben sunk back into his seat, too car sick to argue with her.

"Jeez, babe. Lighten up," Lexx chimed in.

"Listen. I am not your 'babe.' And no, I won't lighten up. It was reckless and stup-"

"She's right guys."

Everyone looked at Jeremy.

"She's right," he reiterated. "It was a stupid move and I'll try to think more clearly next time. But for right now we need to get out of here. And that way is west- Oh shit..."

There was a large group of dead several city blocks in front of them blocking the entire road. They had not noticed the Jeep yet, but it wouldn't take much longer.

"Turn down this alley," Tori said, pointing to her right.

Jeremy listened and turned into the back alley. It was littered with dumpsters and trash, but clear enough for the Jeep to fit through. Only problem was it lead them deeper into the city. Everything seemed to be pushing them away from leaving. They came to a small parking lot at the end of the alley. Jeremy pulled the Jeep into the parking lot and brought it to a rest.

"Whoa, why are we stopping?" Tori asked, a look of concern washing over her face.

"Well, it seems that we are low on gas. We must have burned up a good bit when we cut through the park. These cars may still have some in them. If we could find a hose, maybe we could siphon some of it out and get going. But right now, we'll barely make it out of the city," Jeremy said.

"You have got to be kidding me," she said.

"Wish I was."

"Awesome. Where are we going to find a hose?" She sighed.

"What about over there?" Ben said.

He pointed across the street towards the Savannah College of Arts and Design building. Painted on one of the windows was "shopSCAD". It was easy to read because someone boarded up the windows with plywood.

"Maybe there's a hose in there?" He asked out loud.

"Could be man, you can never tell with SCAD," Jeremy said with a smile.

"Alright! Let's go check it out then!" Lexx said, ready to get back on the road and still pumped from the ride through the park.

They checked the surrounding area for zombies before exiting the Jeep. Gathering up their weapons, Jeremy and Ben decided to leave their pistols in the Jeep. Tori and Lexx would handle the firearms. Lexx with his shotgun and Tori with her pistol. It seemed clear for the most part, so they made their way across the street.

"Looks like somebody tried to board this place up," Lexx whispered.

"Yeah, you think someone's in there?" Ben asked.

"Maybe. If so the door's probably locked."

The door was unlocked. Ben looked at Lexx who only shrugged. They walked into the building and closed the door quietly behind them. Lexx turned the deadbolt on the door once they were all inside. The group looked at him.

"Just in case."

The main room was large and open. It was filled with all sorts of SCAD merchandise and school supplies. Like most SCAD buildings, this was a restored historical building. So, while from the outside it looked like something from Savannah's past, the inside was a mix of modern and antebellum architecture.

"Well, we should probably split up," Tori said.

"Uh, I vote no," Ben chimed in.

"Why?"

"Well, this may sound silly, but given our recent situation, nothing really sounds too absurd. I don't think we should split up because, whenever people split up in horror movies, well, the black guy dies. And I don't know if you noticed, but, um, I'm black..."

Lexx and Jeremy started laughing uncontrollably. Tori just stared at Ben, shaking her head.

"Are you serious right now?"

"I know, I know. Look, if you had asked me that a couple of days ago, the thought would have never come to mind. But c'mon, we are basically living in a horror movie right now. Cut me some slack," he answered.

"Oh my god, that is the funniest thing I've heard in a long time," Lexx said, pausing in between chuckles. Tori just shook her head, but a small smile began to creep up around her lips.

"Ok, Ben. We stick together," she said.

"Thank you. I know I may act somewhat white but I don't know how the rules work. If there are even "rules" anymore. Rather not take my chances, y'know?"

She smiled and nodded.

"Ok. Let's find some hose."

Her saying this only made Lexx and Jeremy take one look at each other and laugh even harder.

"What is so damn funny?" she asked.

"Hey Ben, where da hose at?" Lexx said.

Ben shook his head, furrowing his eyebrows.

"I don't get it. What do you mean?"

"You know man," Lexx started. "Where da hose at? Like, ho's? Pimps and ho's, man. Tori said we should find some ho's."

"You two are idiots," she said.

Ben still looked lost. Lexx stopped laughing.

"Haha, I don't think you have to worry about that whole being black-thing, man," he said to Ben.

Ben gave him a smirk and the finger. Jeremy held up his hand, motioning for everyone to stop. He wiped a few tears from his eyes and got his composure.

"Alright guys. Let's go find *a hose*."

There were a few clicks from behind them.

"Freeze. And drop your weapons," said a shrill, tiny voice.

They all turned and looked to a group of people pointing several rifles and shotguns in their direction.

Chapter Seventeen

"I said freeze!"

The guy speaking was holding what looked like an AK-47. He looked like a guerilla soldier, as he was wearing a mixture of vintage and grungy-looking clothing. He was short, skinny, and wearing black, thick-framed glasses. His goatee was well manicured. It formed a sinister frame for his crooked smile.

The people behind him were also holding guns. They were a mismatched group. Several were wearing clothes like the little guy, hipsters or art students. Black V-necks and skinny jeans. But two of them were decked out in camo hunting gear. The two of them were holding shotguns and stood on each side of the main guy, like bodyguards. Besides the AK and shotguns, Jeremy counted two hunting rifles, and one rather large handgun. These people were very well armed.

"Hey, hey, we don't want any trouble," Jeremy said, holding up both hands in a peace offering.

"Drop the sword then."

Jeremy was still wearing his machete at the waist. He shook his head at the guy's wording, but reached for and lowered the machete. Tori began to protest, but Jeremy gave her a reassuring look, and she backed down. He sat the machete on the ground in front of him and looked back at the guy shouting orders.

"Look," he started again. "We don't want any trouble. We're just looking for some gas, or maybe a hose to siphon some gas. We're not looking for a place to stay or anything else."

The little guy walked up to Jeremy, giving him the look over. He reeked of clove cigarettes and cheap beer, most likely beer Jeremy had never heard of. After circling around Jeremy, he stopped in front of him and looked him in the face.

"My name is Albert. And this is our home."

The word *home* caused both him and his friends to giggle. Something was off with them. Jeremy looked back to his friends. Lexx mouthed the word, "Homeless?"

Jeremy shook his head and mouthed back, "Hipsters."

Lexx grimaced. He hated hipsters.

"We don't have any gas for you," Albert continued. "And you can't siphon any gas. That would be stealing."

Again the group giggled like school children. If they were trying to make Jeremy feel uneasy, they were succeeding. The whole situation seemed off. Something deeper was going on here.

"We'd like for your friends to give us their weapons now," Albert said, his voice monotone and calm.

He motioned his rifle towards the others. Tori had her 9mm drawn, finger on the trigger. Lexx was holding the shotgun; Ben his hand on his hatchet.

"We're not giving you our weapons," Tori said.

"You don't really have a choice, do you? We have much more superior firepower than you do. I'm sure your friend's hatchet there is good for the dead, but it won't do much against Agatha here."

Albert held up his AK, bringing it to his lips and planting a kiss on the barrel.

"Agatha? That's a stupid name," Lexx mumbled.

"It was my grandmother's name!" Albert shouted, pointing the gun in Lexx's direction. His voice changed from shrill shriek to a deep thundering.

"Did I say stupid? I meant that's a great name. My bad," Lexx said.

Everyone stood in silence for a moment.

"Look, we'll just walk right back out, and leave you here to do, well, whatever it is you're doing here," Jeremy finally spoke.

"That's just not going to work for us. You see, you

know where we are, and well, you could come back and steal from us. Or hurt us. I won't allow you to do that. Take their weapons," Albert answered, motioning for the two camo guys to relieve Jeremy and the others of their weapons.

They didn't hesitate, like dogs to their master's bidding. They walked over and took the two guns, the hatchet, and Jeremy's machete. Jeremy wished that they had brought the other two pistols, but they were still in the Jeep. Tori started to put up a fight, but Jeremy again gave her a look that told her to relax. She did, and begrudgingly let the guy take her pistol.

"Good, good," Albert said. "Now we can be friends. Take the men to the holding room. The girl, she's a pretty one. Anastasia, why don't you take her to my room and get her cleaned up. The three of us might have to play later."

He motioned for the one woman of the group, who was holding the pistol, to go over and get Tori. Her face at first seemed upset by Albert's new interest in Tori, but she quickly hid it with a smile. She held the gun to Tori's back and pushed her towards the stairs. Jeremy watched as the woman escorted her upstairs. Tori looked pissed.

"I just want you to know," Lexx spoke up. "This will go badly for you in the end."

Albert smiled and walked away.

"Lock them up. The big one especially."

***

"What the fuck are we going to do?"

Lexx flexed trying to break free of the rope that he was tied up with.

"First, you have to calm down," Jeremy answered.

"You're not going to be any good to us if you're too tired to do anything if we do get out."

They were in some kind of supply room or closet. The walls were lined with shelves, filled with store merchandise, and other supplies. The room was dim, a single light bulb flickered light from the ceiling. Jeremy looked around, his eyes adjusting to the darkness, trying to look for something of use.

"I see some scissors up on one of the shelves, but from where I am, I can't reach them," said a voice in the darkness.

"Who is that?" Lexx asked. "Who are you?"

"My name is Avery. These freaks took me captive too."

"How did you get here Avery?" Jeremy asked.

"I was skating down in the park when things started going bad. I ducked in here to stay safe and these guys jumped me. Started spouting off nonsense about the end of the world and a new world order. Personally, I think they're all on drugs. Maybe even on alcohol. You guys want some Vienna sausages? I can reach those."

"No, we don't want your soggy ass sausages," Lexx said.

"Your loss," Avery said.

You could hear the slurping of sausage juices in the dark. Jeremy tugged at his ropes, trying to see if there was some sort of weak spot. He fidgeted for a moment. Nothing.

This is not good, he thought. *Not good at all.*

He thought about Tori and what Albert meant by "play". The guy seemed off his rocker and his friends didn't seem any better. They had to get to her.

"Hey Avery," Jeremy said.

"Yes," he answered between sausages.

"There was a woman with us. They took her up to Albert's room. Do you know where that is?"

"I don't know man," Avery said. "I heard the girl, Anastasia, talk about it. She's the one they send in to check on me. Nice girl, except for the fact she hangs out with these lunatics. Oh, and she's banging Albert. Not an attractive trait, y'know?"

He paused for a sausage.

"Sweet Jesus man, how many of those things do you have?" Jeremy asked.

"There's a couple of packs still down here. Not sure what I'm gonna do when I run out, these are the only food I've had since I've been here. I feel a poop coming on too. That's gonna be real interesting. Being tied up and all."

"Did she say anything about the room?" Lexx interrupted.

"No, not really. Except that's where they have sex. She told me a lot about their sex life. Way too much. She must get bored because she comes in here and tells me stuff. Gross stuff if you ask me. No, she didn't say much about the room, except that there was an outside balcony. She said they did it there. In front of the zombies. Weird, right?"

"If he touches her..." Lexx said.

"Stay calm, Lexx," Jeremy said. "Avery, do you know why Albert is the one in charge? He just doesn't seem to fit the role of leader."

"Totally. Yeah, Albert wasn't originally the one in charge. It was some guy named Richie. He was one of the hunters, who shacked up here in the building. I'm sure you've met his two lackeys, Hank and Clay? Well, according to Anastasia, Richie thought he'd be the one in charge, so he was bossing everybody around, and just being a real dick about everything. When Albert and Anastasia joined the group, Richie took a liking to Anastasia. He tried to rape her. So, Albert cut his head off. Ever since then, he's been the one in charge."

"That's crazy," Jeremy said, his mouth hanging open.

"Yeah," Avery continued. "He doesn't seem like an alpha male, but when I voiced concern about his methods of offing Richie, he locked me in here. Which, I guess, is a lot better than getting my head cut off."

Lexx was still squirming in his ropes.

"I'm fucking serious! If that psychopath touches one hair on her head..."

"Don't worry man; I'll have you out of here in a jiffy."

"What?" Lexx said, surprised to see Ben standing in front of him. He had the scissors in hand and began to cut Lexx loose.

"How did you get out?" Lexx and Jeremy both asked at nearly the same time.

"Eh, old magician's trick. I studied a little magic when I was younger. Went through this whole phase where I wanted to be a magician. If you tense up real tight when someone ties you up and then later relax, the ropes should be loose enough for you to escape. Houdini did it all the time."

"Harry fucking Houdini!" Lexx said.

Jeremy started laughing.

"You've got a few tricks up your sleeves don't you, Ben?" Jeremy asked.

Ben smiled.

"Now, let's get you out of here."

Chapter Eighteen

Tori was seething as she squirmed to free herself from the ropes around her ankles and wrists. Anastasia had tied her to an antique chair and left her alone in the large room. There were several couches, chairs, and a single mattress lying on the floor; the room had been made into a living area. To her right, Tori could see a glass door leading to a balcony. If she could get free, maybe she could get out there, and climb down the side of the building. She thought of the pistols in the Jeep, but the tightness of the ropes rubbing against her bare skin brought her thoughts back to the present.

That girl Anastasia may be dumb as a bag of bricks, she thought, *but she sure can tie her knots. I'll give her that much.*

As if hearing her name, Anastasia walked back into the room, holding a towel draped over her arm and a smile on her face. Her smiling only made Tori more enraged. Anastasia did not seem to notice or care, as she kneeled down in front of Tori.

"Sorry, we don't have any warm water. This will just have to do," she said as she began to wipe dirt and grime from Tori's face.

"Why are you doing this?" Tori asked. "I mean, what's in this for you? Obviously, the two of you are together. It doesn't bother you he wants me now too? That you're not enough?"

Anastasia stopped for a few seconds to ponder Tori's words, but then resumed her cleaning. She began to whistle.

"I think it's pretty fucked up," Tori continued. "You saw the way he looked at me. You're not enough for him. What do you even see in that guy anyway? He seems like a total dork, much less a leader."

"He is a dork. But he's my dork," Anastasia said

calmly.

"Why do you even stay here? For protection? Help us, and we can protect you, Anastasia," Tori tried to persuade.

"How will you protect me? You don't have anywhere safe to live. You're just wandering around in a silly, old Jeep with no gas," she said, continuing to clean.

The girl's voice was dull, emotionless. Tori's words seemed to go in one ear and right out the other. She had to argue facts.

"We're heading west. Less people, less zombies. Think about it. It'll be safe there. You're just a piece of meat to these guys. When Albert's done with you, who knows what these other guys will do with you."

"He told me he loved me."

"Of course he said that!" Tori yelled, rolling her eyes. "You're the only girl here! Think honey, the second I showed up or another girl shows up, you're history."

Anastasia stood up and turned her back to Tori.

"Don't say that."

"You have to know it's true," Tori continued to press. "But you can help us. You can make a difference. You can help us get out of here."

Tori waited to see if Anastasia would respond. There was no way she could just ignore common sense. She didn't look that naïve. She looked to be around the same age as Tori. She was too old to be hung up on a guy like that. Anastasia began to snivel.

Hopefully she's getting it and thinking it over, Tori thought.

Anastasia turned back around. She was smiling.

"Nice try bitch. Did you really think I'm that big of a twit?" Anastasia said.

Tori was shocked at the sudden change in the girl's demeanor.

"What?" Tori asked. "So, you're going to help us?"

"Help you?" Anastasia laughed. "Hell no! I'm not sure what I want to do with you yet, but I'm sure I'll figure out a good use for all of you! I especially know what I want to do with that bigger fellow with you. He looked rather tasty."

Tori was confused.

"What do you mean that *you'll* figure out something to do?"

Anastasia laughed again.

"Well, you had one thing right blondie, Albert is no leader."

She walked away from Tori and the chair over to a bag sitting near the mattress.

"You see, before you got here, there was another guy who thought he'd be king of this castle. Well, he got a little rambunctious. And that is never a good thing. Well, when Albert and myself got here, this guy wanted to repopulate the planet. With me. I, of course, kindly declined his offer. He didn't like that."

She pauses in her searching for a moment, as if to think about what to say next.

"He," she continued. "He took us up to this room and tied Albert to that chair you're sitting in. He was going to make Albert watch as he raped me."

Tori's stomach turned.

"But that didn't happen."

She stood up and was holding something in front of her. Tori couldn't see what it was from where she was sitting. Anastasia slowly turned around. Tori gasped.

"It didn't happen, because I CUT HIS FUCKING HEAD OFF!"

Held in her right hand by the hair was the decapitated head of the man she was talking about. Its eyes were rolled back up into its skull and slack jawed mouth agape. The blood had dried around the neck, but the occasional drip of dark red liquid fell to the floor.

"You're out of your fucking mind!" Tori yelled.

Anastasia took the head and reared back like a bowler. She sent the head rolling across the floor, all the way out onto the balcony. She smiled.

"Maybe," she said. "Anyways, I knew that if the other's found out I cut off poor little Richie's head, they'd kill me. But, if they found out it was Albert, they'd be afraid. You see, my brother may not be many things, but he can be a very convincing actor."

"Why keep us here then?" Tori again asked, trying to get the conversation back.

"Isn't it obvious? Both Albert and myself were hoping another girl would come along. He's not the only one wanting fresh meat. I like girls too. Especially the way they taste. And well, that turns him on."

Tori rolled her eyes. This girl was completely psycho.

"You're pathetic," she said. "And just know that when you let me out of these ropes to play, the only thing you'll be tasting is blood from when I punch you in your pretty little mouth."

"Ooh. Feisty. I like that," Anastasia responded.

Anastasia planted a kiss on the top of Tori's head and just continued to smile. She walked over to a table in the corner of the room and sifted through what looked to be a suitcase.

"Let's see," she said. "We're going to have to dress you up a bit. I notice you're not wearing a bra. Not a problem. One of mine should fit you just fine. We're going to have to boost the girls up just a bit for Albert. He like's 'em plump."

"How you going to get my shirt off without untying me?" Tori asked. "Cause I can promise you, the second these ropes come off, you're dead."

Anastasia giggled to herself. She walked back over to Tori. She was holding the towel, a pink push-up bra and a large kitchen knife. The blade was stained in dried blood. She took the towel and gagged Tori with it, leaning in real close to her ear.

"Well," she giggled. "We're just going to have to cut that shirt off then, aren't we?"

***

"Alright Avery, where are we going?"

Jeremy turned back to look at Avery. He was around Jeremy's age, maybe a year younger. He was wearing a striped tank top and some cargo shorts. He looked like he was headed to the beach rather than skateboarding.

"There's a service elevator in the back. We can use that to get upstairs."

"How do you know that?" Ben asked.

"The girl would use it when she would come to check on me. One time she left the door open long enough for me to see her use it. I know it's there."

They walked down the hallway quietly although nobody seemed to be around. When they came to the end, Avery pointed to an abnormally narrow doorway. He mouthed the word "elevator," and motioned up with his thumb. Jeremy nodded, and checked to see if the coast was clear. He saw no one so he walked over to the door while the others waited.

There was a button on the wall with no markings.

That has to be it, Jeremy thought.

He pressed it, and the door slid open.

Ding.

They all cringed. It wasn't really that loud, but against the backdrop of silence, it was deafening. Jeremy waited for someone to come out and investigate the noise, but no one came. He looked back to the others with a shrug, and then motioned for them to come over to the elevator.

"There's no way all of us are gonna fit in that tiny thing," Lexx whispered.

He was right. It would maybe hold two of them. It was obviously a retrofit and not a piece of the original building.

"You're right," Jeremy said. "You go get her. Me and Avery will go out this door, and circle around to the Jeep. We'll get the pistols out of there and come back in to get y'all. Ben, you stay by this door so we can get back in. Hang on to those scissors."

Ben looked down at the large sewing shears he was still holding and nodded.

"Alright, sounds like a plan," Lexx said. "Make it quick. Things might get dicey."

Jeremy nodded as Lexx got in the elevator and the door slid shut.

***

"Question: Why aren't we just getting out of here? Why go back inside?" Avery asked, as they snuck around the building towards the Jeep.

"We have to go back in and get our guns. I thought about leaving them, but with those crazy, runner zombies, I'd like to have the firepower if needed. Maybe we can snag some of their weapons while we're in there too. I sure wouldn't mind the extra firepower," Jeremy answered, trying to keep his voice down.

"Oh man," Avery said. "So you think they're zombies too? I thought I was the only one who figured it out."

"That's just what we're calling them. We don't know for sure," Jeremy said, still trying to keep his voice down. He hoped Avery would get the hint and keep his down too.

"These are definitely zombies man, no doubt about

it-"

"Avery, keep your voice down," Jeremy interjected.

There were a few zombies littered around the surrounding area. Avery nodded and put a finger up to his lips. He figured it out. The dead seemed unaware of their voices.

The building itself was situated on one of Savannah's famous squares. Having survived the Civil War, much of the original colonial layout was still very much a part of the city. It seemed that while General Sherman thought it would be fun to torch the rest of the South, he decided Savannah was too beautiful, and presented it to President Lincoln as a Christmas present. If he could only see it now.

Most of the zombies were wandering around the square. A mix of undead tourists and locals. The weather was beautiful this afternoon. Not a cloud in the sky and a cool breeze kept the air a pleasant temperature. Perfect for an afternoon downtown. The dead didn't seem to notice the two men slinking along the building's edge.

"Good thing they boarded the windows. They can't see us from inside. That's dumb. You'd think they'd want to be able to see outside," Avery rambled, forgetting the whole "be quiet" thing.

"Dude, shut up," Jeremy hushed him.

Avery nodded and made a motion of zipping his lips. He placed the imaginary key in his pocket.

This guy sure does talk a lot, Jeremy thought to himself. *But no doubt, he has been helpful so far*.

Jeremy wanted to ask Avery questions about himself, to get to know him better, but he'd already told him to be quiet twice. Didn't want to contradict that. The guy did not seem to have a volume control on his voice. Jeremy will just have to wait to find out more about him.

They made their way over across the street without

being seen by any of the dead. Jeremy ducked down next to the Jeep and tried to open the door as quietly as he possibly could. There was a faint click, but it didn't draw any unwanted attention. He reached in and picked up the two pistols from the center console. His backpack sat in between the two front seats. He grabbed that too. They might need it to carry spare ammo or other supplies. They still had to find a hose too.

Turning to Avery he whispered, "Can you handle one of these?"

Avery nodded, reaching out for the gun. They turned to make their way back to the building when Jeremy noticed a balcony outside a second story window. It was the only one on the building. He pointed up to the balcony.

"Is that the one you were talking about?" He asked Avery.

Avery nodded.

"Are you sure?"

He nodded again, slower this time. Jeremy noticed he didn't look too confident.

"Is it or is it not?" he whispered through his teeth.

Avery held up his hands and shrugged.

"Why aren't you talking?"

Avery reached into his pocket and pulled out the imaginary key from earlier. He put it up to his mouth and gave it a twist.

"You told me to shut up."

Jeremy was dumbfounded.

"Are you serious?" He asked, shaking his head in disbelief.

"Mostly. Yeah, I don't know for sure if that is the balcony she was talking about, but I don't see any others so that has to be it," he said, this time keeping his voice low.

Jeremy turned and looked up at the balcony.

"Tori?" He whispered, just loud enough for her to hear if she was there, but not loud enough for any zombies to take notice.

Nothing.

"Tori? You there?" He said, this time a little louder.

Again nothing.

"Tori?"

Again a little louder and again no answer. A zombie in the square moaned. It had noticed the two men near the building and was beginning to limp its way over to them, grabbing the attention of others as well.

"C'mon man, let's go," Avery insisted. "Maybe she just can't hear you."

Jeremy nodded. They turned to run back to the door where Ben waited on the inside, but as they started, a figure walked out onto the balcony.

It was Anastasia.

"Oh boys, you should have stayed inside," she giggled. "Zombies! Come and get it!"

Chapter Nineteen

Lexx wandered the upstairs hallway.
All the doors are closed, he thought. *Which one is it?*
"Zombies! Come and get it!"
He heard the girl yell from the closed door right beside him. Quickly, he opened the door, and there was Tori tied to a chair with her shirt cut in two right down the middle. The girl, Anastasia, was standing out on the balcony. She whipped around once Lexx opened the door.
"You too?" she asked, before yelling for help.
Lexx charged in and ran straight for the girl. She was still holding the kitchen knife that she had been scrap-booking Tori's shirt with. As Lexx got closer, she waved it back and forth in front of her.
"Get back!"
Lexx ignored her, pushed the knife out of the way, and shoved the girl out onto the balcony. He then closed the door, and locked it, leaving her banging on the glass to get back in. She let out a string of obscenities.
"That girl has a pretty foul mouth on her," he said, as he causally walked over to Tori. Anastasia in the background continued her assault of banging and swearing on the balcony door.
"You have no idea," Tori said.
This was the second time today she was relieved to see that man. When she saw the truck explode earlier, she was just sad that he died. He had become a friend and a trusted partner in this whole apocalypse deal. Now, she was honestly happy that it was Lexx that came to get her, and not one of the others. Nothing against the other guys, but Lexx was indeed starting to grow on her.

Damnit, she thought, as he began to untie the rope from around her ankles. His rough hands gently slid over the bare skin of her lower legs.

She gave him a good look over as he worked to liberate her from the chair.

He's not bad looking, she thought.

His rugged features and solid frame really overshadowed his slightly receding hairline. His five o'clock stubble was filling in his jaw line quite nicely too.

Good Lord, what am I thinking? She thought.

Once her hands were free, they shot down to rub where the ropes had been.

"Thank you," she said.

"Rescue's not over yet babe," Lexx answered.

He stood up and began to look for anything he could use as a weapon.

"Well, locking her out there was a good idea. That girl is bat-shit crazy," Tori said as she joined in the search. She walked over to Anastasia's suitcase. Not a single thing to be used as a weapon. There were some large, rubber "devices," but those probably would not do much damage against the skull of a walking corpse.

"Yeah, I guess so," Lexx said. "My first idea was to just dropkick her off the balcony, but then I thought, *You don't just dropkick girls off the balcony.* So, I locked her out there instead."

"Good thinking. Holy crap! Look at this thing," she said, holding up one of the larger rubber phalluses.

"Looks small to me," Lexx said with a shrug.

She looked over at him. He paused long enough to give her a quick smile, but went back to looking. After a few minutes of frantic searching, they both gave up.

"Nothing," he said. "Didn't she have a pistol earlier? Where is it?"

Tori did one last glance over the room. Anastasia had stopped banging on the door and was crumpled down on the balcony crying. She was holding the large kitchen knife to her chest, like a small child would with a stuffed animal, or security blanket.

"Hold on a sec," Tori said.

She walked over to the balcony door and unlocked it. As she opened the door, Anastasia jumped up to her feet.

"Oh, thank you, thank you," she began crying.

"Give me the knife," Tori said.

Anastasia held the knife back up to her chest and shook her head. She acted like a toddler who did not want to give up her toy. Tori could see over the rail and saw the amassing crowd of dead at street level.

"Give me the knife, or we leave you here. With them," she said, motioning towards the zombies below.

Anastasia shook her head more violently and sprung at Tori, knife pointed straight for her gut. In one fluid move, Tori grabbed her by the wrist, and twisted. The knife fell to the ground. She held her arm firmly, pulled her in close, and looked her in the eyes. The girl flicked out her tongue in a seductive way.

"No thanks," she said as she shoved the girl back and planted her foot right square into her chest.

Anastasia went spiraling back towards the balcony railing, arms flailing. She lost her balance and tumbled head first into the moans of the dead below. Tori went to grab her before she went over, but missed her by a nanosecond. Anastasia's screams grew louder as the crowd of zombies began to devour her. She kicked and screamed, but fell silent when one of the zombies reached its dead grey fingers into her mouth, and ripped her jaw from its hinge.

Tori stood there in disbelief. She did not mean for that to happen. She tried to grab the girl, but it was too late.

"I, I didn't mean to kick her off, just back," she stammered.

Lexx walked over and picked up the knife. He placed a hand on Tori's shoulder, trying to comfort her, and to pull her back into reality.

"I believe you babe. But what's done is done, let's go," he said softly.

She nodded hesitantly and turned to go back in the building.

"However," he added. "I guess you *can* just kick girls off the balcony."

She punched him in the arm.

"Shut up. Let's go. Someone is bound to come investigate all the noise. Let's find Jeremy and Ben and get the hell out of here."

She started to walk to the door.

"Um, Tori?"

"Yeah, what?" She snapped.

"You, uh, maybe wanna grab a new shirt?"

Lexx pointed to her half cut open shirt. She looked down and saw that her breasts were pretty well exposed from where Anastasia cut her shirt. She never put the bra on either, so Tori was pretty much going girls gone wild. A new shirt might have not been such a bad idea.

"Why? You don't like this look on me?" she said coyly.

"I love this look on you."

She giggled. A few shirts could be seen hanging out of Anastasia's bag, so Tori walked over and inspected a few. She picked one that seemed to be clean. She took off the tattered mess she was wearing, ignoring Lexx's dropped jaw, and put on the white cotton shirt that read, "I 'heart' Savannah". Instead of a heart, a peach was in its place. She put her hands on her hips and faced Lexx.

"How do I look?"

"You workin' it girl," Lexx said, snapping his fingers in a z-formation.

She laughed again and he smiled at her, their eyes

catching for a brief moment. The smile faded from Tori's face as she pulled herself together.

"Alright, let's get the hell out of here."

***

Ben quickly opened the door for Jeremy and Avery when they started to relentlessly bang on the door. There was a small group of z's behind them, one right on their heels. It reached out with its rotting arm as Ben went to slam the door shut, getting it caught between the door and doorframe. It moaned in a painful agony, which caught Ben off guard, because until now, he had not noticed any of the dead even register pain. He slammed the door again. Crunch. Again. Crunch. He slammed it a fourth time, this time with a sickening crack, successfully separating bone and tendon. The dead forearm fell to the floor; its fingers still grasping for a brief moment, until finally succumbing to death.

"Shit, shit, shit," Ben muttered under his breath.

He looked over at Jeremy and Avery, who were both hunched over, trying to regain their breath. Jeremy straightened up, taking a deep breath.

"We need to find Lexx and Tori and get out of here. Pronto," he said.

"What was that scream?" Ben asked.

"I think it was that girl," Avery said. "I think someone threw her off the balcony."

"Oh, geez," Ben said. "You think Lexx did that? Why would he do that? Her friends are not going to be happy."

Jeremy shook his head.

"Let's hope not."

He motioned for them to follow him. They turned a corner and began to walk down the corridor. Modern art lined the walls. None of it made any sense to

Jeremy.

I could make that, he thought. *It just looks like someone threw paint against a canvas.*

He was lost deep in thought when they rounded a corner, running right smack into Albert and two of his men. Everyone drew their weapons. A good old fashioned Mexican stand-off. Albert was still holding "Agatha" and the two camo guys were with him, who were still holding their shotguns.

"What are you doing out?" Albert stammered. "What was that scream? Where did you get guns?"

Jeremy held his ground. He glanced over at Avery. The kid was sweating bullets, but had his pistol ready and pointed for one of the shotgun guys. Jeremy mouthed a "ssh"; Avery nodded. Ben was still holding the scissors he found earlier. Albert definitely had the upper hand.

"Who screamed?" Albert said, his voice much sterner this time

"Your girl," Jeremy said.

"What? Anastasia? What did you do to her?"

The two guys with Albert looked at each other, both now looked more nervous than confident in their leader.

"WHAT DID YOU DO?" Albert bellowed, his voice now no longer nasally and meek.

"We threw her off the balcony," Jeremy answered.

Ben shot him a look as if to say, "What are you doing?"

Jeremy ignored it.

"You what?"

"We threw her off the balcony into a group of zombies."

Albert twitched as he processed the information. Tears started to well up in the corners of his eyes. Jeremy grew nervous as he watched the man's finger tighten around the trigger. Albert began to snivel, but quickly stopped. His face darkened, anger taking over. He straightened up, pointing the barrel of the AK-47 directly for Avery.

"DIE!" he screeched.

Jeremy shoved Avery hard right before Albert began unloading his clip into the wall behind where Avery stood. The bullets ran up the wall as the rifle jumped in Albert's hands, the barrel rising with each shot. Jeremy dove for the ground and fired his pistol hitting the left shotgun guy in the shoulder. This caused him to misfire his shotgun blasting his buddy with buckshot. Albert's rifle finally ran out of ammo, his war cry trailing off into a whimper. He lowered his gun and looked to see his back-up lying on the ground. His bravado now gone, he turned back to face Jeremy and the others. The front of his pants turned dark with urine.

"You've never fired a gun before have you?" Avery said as he stood up, dusting himself off.

Albert sheepishly shook his head no.

"Dude," Avery said. "Yuhdum."

Albert turned and ran.

Chapter Twenty

They followed after Albert, who led them into the main room where everything started. He ran and hid behind the other two guys who were standing there with rifles drawn. These two were the ones dressed in skinny jeans and deep V-neck t-shirts. If the camo guys looked like they knew what they were doing, these two had no idea. As he positioned himself behind them, his crooked smile crept back up. Jeremy, Avery, and Ben came to a halt and raised their new shotguns. Ben was dual-wielding the two pistols, trying to look like he knew what he was doing.

"Albert," Jeremy started, again holding out one hand as a peace offering. "Just let us go. Get some help for your people, and just let us go."

The small man smiled for a minute and then laughed.

"Kill them," he said.

His two cronies hesitantly aimed their rifles and prepared to fire. Jeremy could tell that they did not want to kill anyone, but that they also did not want to cross Albert. He had no idea what made these people blindly follow him. Their fingers tightened around the triggers. Everyone held their breath.

"Not today, bitches!"

Lexx came flying off the second floor balcony, a knife in his right hand. He came down on one of the rifle-hipsters, who tried to aim the barrel up at the falling man, but only ended up taking a knife across the chest. The blade cut through the shoulder strap, sending the gun to the floor. His friend went to fire at Lexx, but Tori came up behind him, putting him in a choke-hold. She had snuck down the stairs and flanked

Albert and his men. The guy's face turned blue and he quickly passed out. She let him fall to the floor with a thud. He lay there motionless next to his bleeding buddy, who just groaned in pain.

Albert realized he was now completely surrounded. Surrounded by people he had really, really pissed off. His friend's knife wound was not going to kill him, but that guy was not getting up to protect Albert anytime soon. The cards were greatly stacked against him.

"I knew you would harm us," he said quietly.

Tori kicked him in the back of the knee, causing his legs to buckle, and put him sprawled out on the floor.

"You put this shit upon yourself!" Tori yelled. "Don't you dare put that on us. You should have just let us go!"

Jeremy held up his hand, motioning that was enough. She nodded and backed off. He handed his shotgun to Tori, and crouched down next to Albert, looking him in the face. Albert's head raised a little to meet Jeremy's gaze.

"What?" he huffed.

Jeremy continued to stare at the man. Albert hung his head low again.

"Are you going to kill me?"

"No," Jeremy answered. "But I am going to ask you again, do you have any gasoline?"

Albert began to giggle again. The man was losing it. He began to shake his head violently, much like Anastasia did earlier. Tori raised her shotgun.

"No gas. No gas. No gas," he began to mumble over and over.

Jeremy stood back up and shrugged his shoulders.

"I think we've lost him," he said. "Let's just go-"

"HELP! NO, NO, GET AWAY!"

Yelling came from the hallway. The guy who Jeremy shot in the shoulder came running out. He held his hand on his wound. Blood stained his camouflage shirt. He lost his footing coming into the room and took a nasty spill, not able to catch himself. He turned over on his back just in time for a mob of zombies to come pouring into the room. The first few fell on him and began to rip into him, tearing away at his flesh.

"NO! NO!"

He kicked at them, but they didn't care. They were hungry.

"Let's go!" Jeremy yelled, running towards the door.

"What about him?" Ben yelled, motioning towards Albert.

"Leave him!" Tori said.

"We can't just leave him," Ben shot back.

She looked at Jeremy to make the call.

"What am I? The decision maker now?" he said.

Lexx got to the door first, but took enough time to retrieve one of the rifles from the floor. He held the door open for them to run through. Avery went through. Tori made a quick bow towards Lexx as she passed him. Ben reached the door next, stopping to look at Albert then to Jeremy.

"We can't just leave the man," Ben said.

Jeremy went to answer him, but noticed that one of the zombies looked familiar. It was a young woman. What was left of her intestines hung from the dark cavity in her stomach. Her mascara was smeared down her face, darkened by blood. She was missing the bottom half of her jaw.

It was Anastasia.

Albert looked up as she shambled towards him, arms reaching out for him. Her left arm must have broken from the fall, because it was bent in an angle that was unnatural. His face lit up.

"Sis," he said. "It wasn't supposed to end this way. I

did everything you said. I did everything just the way you said. Why didn't it work?"

She fell on him and began to peel the skin from her brother's bones. Jeremy looked away and back to Ben. Ben nodded and exited the building.

"I guess that solves that problem," Jeremy mumbled, before walking through the door and slamming it shut.

***

The situation was no better outside. The noise had attracted zombies from all over the place. They covered the square. Anastasia's screams had really attracted the dead to the area.

"Uh, guys?" Lexx said, after butting a geek in the head with his rifle. "I hate to be the bearer of bad news, but we are in the same position we were in few hours ago!"

He was right. The Jeep still had no gas. Jeremy began to think about how far they could make it on what gas they still had in the tank. It was mostly fumes. They probably wouldn't make it out of the city. The Jeep was good for a lot of things, but sucked at gas mileage. Tori blasted a zombie who wandered too closely to the group, sending a mist of red against the building.

"Hey, over here!" Avery yelled.

He was standing down by the back alleyway that led behind the building. His waved his hand for them to come to him. They ran in his direction, and as they got close, he ran on down into the alley.

"Come on! Hurry!" he yelled.

"Where are we going?" Jeremy asked.

Avery didn't answer, but led them to a small parking area hidden behind the building. Sitting in it were several, new-looking moped scooters.

"I heard them mention these; we can use them to escape!" Avery said with a smile.

"Scooters?" Tori said, unsure if he was being serious.

"Yeah!"

She looked at Jeremy for confirmation.

"You got any better ideas, Tori?" Jeremy asked.

"Uh, not riding scooters for one."

"Look," Avery started. "I know it doesn't seem like a good idea, like not much protection and all, but what they lack in defense they make up in mobility. You can get around obstacles a lot easier on these things than you would be able to in a car. Plus, gas will last you a lot longer."

"He's got a solid point," Jeremy said.

The rest of the group still looked unsure, but the zombies were starting to funnel their way into the alley so time was limited. They all picked a scooter and took off in the opposite direction of the oncoming horde. Avery let out a 'whoop' once they hit the street. Tori shot a glance at Jeremy, but he was too busy enjoying the wind in his hair.

***

They reached Bay Street with no problems. Avery was right. They were able to maneuver around obstacles much better than with the Jeep. And the scooters had enough get up and go to pass up any skirmishes with the dead. Avoiding the dead was much better than taking them on. Once they got to Bay Street, they came to a rest. The pedestrian signs were still on.

"Walk sign on across Bay Street," the automated sign spoke in a monotone voice.

Tori mimicked the sign, causing the others to smile briefly.

"Avery, we were headed west before this. Rincon, to

be exact. We were going to hole up at Ben's parent's and ride this thing out. I'm sure it'd be ok with him if you tagged along with us," Jeremy said.

"Yeah, that's fine with me. He's been a great help," Ben added.

Avery smiled, but looked back east.

"Well, I appreciate the offer guys. I mean, we make a great team and all, but I really need to head home and see if I can find my parents. Plus, I'm going to try and find my buddy Josh. He was my zombie buddy before all this. We use to watch zombie movies and play video games all the time back when all this stuff was still fiction. He's knows a good bit about zombies and stuff, so I'm sure we could make it through this thing."

"You sure?" Jeremy asked.

Avery nodded.

"Yeah, I should be able to get home with no problems. If you don't mind, I'd like to hang onto the shotgun," he said, holding up the gun.

"That's perfectly fine. Do you want a pistol too?"

"No, this will do for now. Thank you though."

Jeremy reached out to shake Avery's hand. They shook hands and Avery kicked his scooter back on. He nodded to everyone else and drove off towards the islands. Jeremy turned back to the group and switched his bike on.

"Alright, west it is."

Chapter Twenty One

As they passed under the ramp leading up to where the Talmadge Bridge had once been, Tori caught herself looking towards South Carolina across the river. She knew her dad was fine. He was a Marine to the core. He would be fine. She just wished she knew that for sure. Parris Island would be safe, but there was just no way to get there from here. Safety seemed so close, but unobtainable. She tried to refocus her thoughts on something else. The only thing that came to mind was: Lexx.

She didn't know why she felt so attracted to the man. She just met him. She couldn't put her finger on what it was that made him so irresistible. Maybe it was his macho attitude or his bravado. Or maybe it was the fact that he was willing to sacrifice himself for a group of people he just met. She saw characteristics in him that she saw in her father.

Oh, geez, she thought. *I'm attracted to my father.*

She shook the thought out of her head. Dr. Patel, the Base shrink, would have had a field day with that little piece of information. Tori was not even going to take herself down that road. Maybe it was the way Lexx's shirt was tight against his muscular build.

Yeah, let's go with that.

***

Once the road was clear from any nearby undead, Jeremy came to a stop. The others followed suit; they looked to Jeremy for a reason to as why he stopped in the middle of the road. He glanced around quickly and then back to the others.

"I think we should find a place to stay for the night," he said. "We lost a lot of time with those crazy hipsters and it will be dark in a few hours. I wouldn't normally ride through this area at nighttime, so now that all hell has broken loose, I sure don't want to."

"Where do you recommend we stay then?" Tori asked. "In the projects?"

She pointed over to the government housing that sat off in the distant left. To be fair, the buildings were just rebuilt. The old ones, dilapidated and worn down, were demolished, and cleared out for the new ones. So, while they were new projects, they were nonetheless still "the projects."

"Uh, no," Jeremy said.

"Why not? Y'all scared of the ghetto?" Ben interjected, a smile creeping up on his face.

The others looked at him with blank faces.

"Relax! I was just kidding," he said. "I wouldn't stay there either."

"Actually, I was thinking of staying in one of these warehouses," Jeremy continued. "The one last night seemed to work pretty good, minus the whole zombie in the courtyard thing. We'll just have to check the perimeter better this time. We have a few hours to prepare as opposed to last night's midnight shack up."

"Well, which one do you have in mind?" Lexx asked.

Jeremy looked around. There were quite a few to choose from. Savannah had the third largest port on the Eastern seaboard and they were right in its backyard. Warehouses were in no short supply. One side of road was all industrial buildings and the other government housing. Ah, Savannah. They don't show all this on the travel shows on TV.

An older, faded white building caught Jeremy's eye. It was rather square and was surrounded by an eight foot tall chain-link fence. There were stacks of wooden pallets and old oil drums lined against the fence. Jeremy thought they could use those to help barricade and better secure the fences. He looked back to the group, who was waiting for him to say something.

"Let's do that one," he said, pointing to the white building.

No one argued. They all cranked up their bikes and rode into the fenced area. Jeremy was unsure if he liked everyone looking to him for answers. He did not really want to be the leader. He would much rather someone else lead. Everyone was older than him, Lexx and Ben more so. Why did they all look to him?

"You still with us man?" Ben asked.

"Yeah," Jeremy answered. "Just thinking, I guess."

"Well start thinking about how we're going to lock this place down," Tori said.

She playfully punched Jeremy in the arm. It was harder than she intended and Jeremy smiled, rubbing his arm. He pointed over to the pallets and barrels.

"We can probably use those to strengthen the fence a little. Put pallets up against the fence and then barrels behind the pallets. Just to help it from being pushed over. Not a hundred percent sure how to keep the crazy ones out, but I don't think anything will really stop them, y'know?"

"Uh, guys," Lexx said, causing the others to all look at him.

He was standing next to his scooter with the seat pulled up. Underneath it was a compartment and it was filled with two boxes of ammunition. One box of twelve gauge shotgun shells and the other ammo for the 30-06 rifle. They all lit up and opened up their own scooters. Each one had a box of ammunition.

"You have got to be kidding me!" Ben said, laughing as he held up his box of 9mm bullets, the exact kind his and Jeremy's pistols used.

Jeremy couldn't believe it. They only had whatever ammo was in the guns, but once that ran out, they'd have just really fancy bludgeons. Now they might have a chance. Especially against the runners.

"Alright then," Lexx said, his smiling fading. "Enough lollygagging. Let's get this place secure enough to sleep in!"

***

Once they finished with the outside, they made their way into the warehouse. A few random zombies wandered the warehouse, but they were quickly and quietly dispatched with the hand tools. Other than that, the building was empty except for a few offices and a small store front near the street side of the building. The warehouse itself was filled with shelving and boxes of whatever it was they stored there. The labels made no sense to Jeremy. They went into the office area and began to make camp there. There was a small kitchenette area with a fridge and a sink.

"Please tell me they have a Coke in there! Dibs on the Coke!" Lexx said as he ran up to the fridge.

He yanked open the door and there in all its glory was a twelve-pack of Coca-Cola.

"Oh man, oh man, oh man. They're still cold!"

He reached in, pulled one out, and opened it all in one fluid movement. He had it down within a matter of seconds. Tori walked up beside him.

"You gonna share any of those with us?"

"I don't know," he said between belches. "Still thinking about it."

This made her laugh. He smiled and handed her one, before he opened and drank his second. She didn't chug hers, but took a few sips before setting it down. Her attention was fixed on the sink. She walked over to it and paused before reaching for the faucet handle.

Water.

"Yes! Water's still on!" she yelled.

"Yeah, it's still on in the bathroom too," Ben yelled

back from another room.

Tori's face lit up.

"I've got to pee so bad! Move!"

She ran off to the bathroom. Jeremy walked into the kitchen area as she zoomed by. He smiled. It was funny how these things they took for granted yesterday were now precious. A can of Coke, tap water, and working bathrooms. Jeremy just shook his head.

Lexx handed him a Coke.

"Just so you know," Lexx started. "Me voluntarily giving you a Coke means you're alright in my eyes."

"Cool," Jeremy said, as he tilted the can back, chugging the cold, carbonated beverage.

***

Tori and Jeremy were the only ones still awake. Lexx had been the first one to fall asleep, probably crashing from his Coca-Cola induced sugar high. Ben lasted a little longer, but he was also no match for the exhaustion that had come over the group. A small desk lamp gave off enough light to light up the room, but was dim enough to sleep with. Tori leaned back in the office chair she claimed earlier.

"What did you do before all of this Jeremy?"

He looked up at her from his spot on the floor. Her question took him off guard a bit. "Before all this." Was it only yesterday that things were normal?

"I worked at a grocery store. A cashier."

"Oh, that sounds so exciting. Please, tell me more."

He shot her a dirty look.

"You asked..."

She smiled.

"Sorry, sarcasm can be my default sometimes. Especially when I'm exhausted. Don't let me make you feel bad. At least you had a job," she said.

"What? You in school or something?" he said,

straightening himself up.

"I graduated a year ago. Right when I got out is when the economy tanked. People didn't want to hire someone with no experience. Before I went to college, everyone told me that in order to get experience, you needed a degree in something! A lot of good that did me. Now I'm unemployed, living at home with my dad, and really have nothing to show for my life. So, please don't let me make fun of you."

"Well, good thing for this whole zombie apocalypse deal, huh?" Jeremy said, trying to hide the smile creeping up on his lips.

"Aha! I see you too have been trained in the arts of sarcasm and wit!"

They laughed quietly for a moment, before Lexx started to stir. Tori held a finger up to her lips, trying to hold back her own laughter. They waited a few seconds before starting their conversation back up. Lexx lay silent and seemed to have fallen back into a deeper sleep.

"I guess we'll have to be a little quieter," she whispered. "Do you have a girlfriend?"

Jeremy shook his head. His thoughts immediately went to Ashley. He really regretted never working up the courage to ask her out. It was too late for that now.

"There was a girl at work. Never asked her out though. She was the first person I saw attacked," he answered.

"Oh. Sorry."

"No, it's alright. We weren't even really friends. I just never worked up the nerve to ask her out."

"So, have you ever had a girlfriend?"

"Yeah. One. Total bitch though. Cheated on me. Repeatedly. We broke up and got back together throughout most of high school. Beginning of senior year though, there was this nasty rumor going around about her blowing one of the baseball players in the dugout. It was the final straw, so I broke up with her for good."

"Oh, wow."

"Yeah, turns out the rumor wasn't all the way true."

"Oops. What did you do then?"

"Nothing. Turns out, she was blowing the *entire* baseball team."

"Wow," Tori said. "That's almost impressive."

They both laughed.

"Alright Dr. Drew, stop grilling me on my love life. What about you? Boyfriend?"

Tori laughed again.

"I had a few, but once they realized how independent I was, it didn't take long for them to hit the road. I was actually waiting for a blind date when everything went to shit."

She looked over to Lexx.

"You like him don't you?"

"What? No!" she said, slightly raising her voice.

"Tori likes Lexx, Tori likes Lexx," Jeremy began to chant quietly in sing-song.

"What are you six? Shut up!"

"You *love* him," he said in the most annoying voice he could make.

"Shut up. I will shoot you."

She started to mock-reach for her gun sitting on the office desk, when a crash came from out in front of the building. They both looked at each other as the ruckus grew louder. There were moans. And a lot of yelling and swearing.

Chapter Twenty Two

Tori kicked Lexx, as she grabbed the shotgun off the desk and ran towards the front.

"Get up!" she yelled.

"Huh? What?" the man said in a half-awake stupor.

But she was already gone. Jeremy was right behind her, rifle in hand. They did not wait for Lexx and Ben to wake up. The commotion out front was getting louder. Profanity-laced yelling filled the air. When they reached the boarded-up front door, Tori pressed her ear up against it.

"There's someone out there. Someone alive," she said.

She looked back at Jeremy to see what they should do. Lexx and Ben came into the room.

"What the hell is going on?" Lexx stammered, holding his side.

"Ssh! Someone's outside. Sounds like they're in trouble," Tori said.

"So? What do you want to do about it?" Lexx asked back.

Again, she looked to Jeremy. He ran his hand through his hair, his mind racing on what to do. They very easily could just not do anything. That would be safe. But it would also be extremely shady. Jeremy couldn't picture himself just leaving someone to die. His mind went to the Padre. The Padre could have left Jeremy on the side of the road to fend for himself, but he took him in. Not only that, but he died so Jeremy could escape. He risked his life twice for someone he didn't know.

I'll be damned if I won't do the same, he thought.

"Lexx, you and Ben come with me. Tori, you wait by this door and when you hear the signal, open it, and get them inside," Jeremy commanded.

"What signal?" she asked.

"I don't know, something loud!" he yelled, as he and the other men ran for the back door.

***

Once they got outside, Jeremy looked over their improvised wall of pallets against the fence and was surprised by what he saw. In the midst of a growing swarm of the dead, was one man.

One.

Now granted, the man was huge. Probably six and half feet easy, the man's large frame towered over most of the dead. He sported a full beard and was wearing a light blue, button-down work shirt. Jeremy couldn't make out what the name tag said. The weapon he was using looked to be one of those emergency fire axes from the glass cases that say, 'Break in Case of Emergency.'

I guess this could be considered an emergency, Jeremy thought.

The man swung it with deadly accuracy. Zombies fell like timber left and right. Limbs and appendages were flying. One zombie got close only to receive the butt end of the handle before the axe head came crashing down on its skull. Grey matter flew out from the opening. The man yanked the axe from the zombie's brain and swung wide, catching two others who seemed to be just too close for comfort.

"Damn. I don't think this guy even needs our help," Lexx said. "He looks like a fuckin' lumberjack out there."

Ben let out a chuckle as the three men watched on as the "Lumberjack" laid waste to the dead around him. They just kept coming and he just kept chopping them down. One down. Another. And another. The bodies were starting to fill the street. But their numbers weren't slowing down. They seemed to be coming from the direction of the housing projects. Jeremy could see a large group of them making their way over to the scene. Perhaps twenty or so.

I don't care who you are, Jeremy thought. *There's no way to defend yourself against twenty of them at once.*

"Ben, how are you with a rifle?" he said out loud.

"I'm a card carrying member of the NRA, so pretty good. Once deer season opens, me and my dad are out there every weekend. Got plenty of meat in the freezer to back it up."

"Good," Jeremy said. "Take the rifle and go find yourself a place where you can see the street over the fence. Lexx come with me."

Jeremy handed the rifle to Ben and motioned for Lexx to follow him. Earlier that day, he noticed that a few of the barrels still had something in them. He wasn't sure what the liquid was, but the sides of the barrels said they were flammable. They put them off to the side of the yard, out of the way of any danger.

"My plan is," he said turning to Lexx. "Take one of those barrels with stuff in it and get it up over the fence. We'll roll it out over the street away from the guy. Once it gets far enough away and maybe draws some of the z's towards it, Ben will take the shot and we'll find out exactly how flammable that stuff is."

Lexx nodded with a large grin and began rolling the barrel to the fence. Jeremy relayed the plan to Ben real quick, who was perched up on a few barrels and hidden behind a pallet. He nodded and took aim towards the street. Jeremy jumped up next to him.

"Hey guy!" he yelled. "Run for the front door!"

The Lumberjack heard him and looked at the front door before bringing his axe down on the neck of a dead woman, separating head from shoulder. He pulled his axe free and began to make his way towards the front door. Jeremy nodded to Lexx and both men lifted the barrel up over their heads and over the fence. It fell with a bang, catching the attention of a few zombies. As it began to roll away from the fence, more noticed, and began to follow it.

Like moths to a flame, Jeremy thought.

It hit the curb on the other side of the four-lane road. Most of the dead had lost interest in the Lumberjack and were now banging on the barrel. The group from the projects was just finally making their way to the street and also began to swarm the barrel.

"You got a shot?" Jeremy shouted to Ben.

He nodded and took a breath. As his finger tightened around the trigger, he felt a bead of sweat run down the side of his face and before it hit the ground, he heard the click of the trigger mechanism.

Boom.

The shockwave of the explosion sent zombie body parts flying and the men ducking for cover. Pieces of rotting, burning flesh rained down from the sky. Jeremy glanced up to see if the Lumberjack was able to get inside. He saw the door swing open and the man make it inside. Tori had apparently gotten the signal.

***

"Thanks," the man said as Lexx handed him a Coke from the fridge.

He sat in one of the office chairs, resting from the frenzy outside.

Even sitting down the man seemed massive, Jeremy thought.

His shirt was drenched in blood. Some was old,

some fresh. He looked to be in his early forties. It was hard to tell with the thickness of his beard.

"What were you doing out there?" Tori asked, finally breaking the tense silence.

He looked at her.

"Not dying."

Tori seemed to realize her question struck a nerve with the man, so she bit her lip, and folded her arms in front of her.

"I think what she meant," Jeremy said, looking at Tori. "How did you end up out there? Where did you come from and why are you traveling the streets at night?"

The man looked at Jeremy. He looked exhausted. Dark circles had formed around the man's eyes. His beard was peppered with grey.

"Look, I haven't slept in two days," the man sighed. "I'll tell you what brought me here, but then I got to get some sleep."

"That seems fair to me," Jeremy said.

The man rested his face in his hands and drew in a deep breath. He rubbed his face and then proceeded to tell his story.

Chapter Twenty Three

"I work at the port. Loading and unloading the shipping containers. I was nearing the end of a twelve-hour shift, fixing to start a double, when a huge tanker came in from Asia somewhere. Not sure where exactly, all those funky letters look the same to me. I overheard someone say China, but I knew for a fact we didn't get anything from the Chinese here.

I was returning from my mandated break, heading back to the lift I worked. The ship was just getting in. It seemed to be cruising pretty fast for the river. The tugs were guiding it in, but it almost seemed like it was picking up speed. Must have been my imagination, cause the thing came to dock with no problems. I was already exhausted before everything went to hell.

Not even sure how it happened. Customs was making a huge deal about the ship and its containers. From where I was seated in the lift, I could see custom's officers arguing with the ship's crew over a few containers. It looked like the custom's guys wanted in, but the crew was refusing. Well, that's just not gonna fly. You ship something into the States from another country, you better be ready for us to take a peek.

It all happened so quick. The container door swung open and those dead freaks started pouring out. The fast ones mostly. You know which ones I mean?"

The Lumberjack looked to the group. They all nodded.

"Yeah, we call them runners," Jeremy said.

"Runners?" said the Lumberjack. "Yeah, I guess that makes sense. We called 'em pinkies, cause of their pink skin compared to the greys. You got a name for the greys?"

Jeremy shook his head.

"Not really, just zombies or z's for short."

"Zombies? Huh, I never thought of that. I guess they are kinda like zombies. Anyways it was a fuckin' bloodbath. Not a lot of guns and shit around the ports, for obvious reasons. Customs had some, but those tools didn't last long. After most of the pinkies ran out, what was left of the greys came tumbling out of the containers. I say what was left of them because it looked like the pinks beat the shit out of them. Anger problems those pinks.

Like I was saying, things went real bad, real quick. Dock workers get this kinda image going for them where they're just these hard-ass, dumb brutes. And to be fair, some of the guys are exactly that. But man, I can't tell you how many grown men I saw just break down and start crying. Grown ass men. They just gave up the will to live. This one kid, who looked young, maybe twenty five, just fell into the fetal position and started sucking his thumb. From where I was sitting, I could see everything. I almost thought about just staying up there where nothing could reach me.

But then I saw the picture of my wife and little girl that I kept in the cab of the lift. I couldn't imagine these things getting to them. They went to my in-laws for the weekend, but what if this wasn't the only place this was happening? I remember fumbling for my phone. I kept getting a busy signal. Everyone must have been trying to call the people they loved by that point. I put the phone back in my pocket and proceeded to climb down from my lift.

When I got ground level, people were running all over the place. The pinks were chasing everyone. The ones that weren't completely ripped to shit came back quickly as more pinks. Well, most of them came back as pinks. There were a few of the more battered ones that went straight into grey mode."

"Grey mode?" Tori asked.

"Yeah, the pink ones eventually tire out and turn into the slower greys. You haven't seen that?"

"No. But then again, we haven't really stuck around to find out," she said.

"Well, I didn't really have much of a choice," the Lumberjack continued. "I met up with my buddy Burton and we were able to find a small maintenance shed to hide out in. A few other people I'd never met joined us. That's where I found this axe."

He holds up the axe before setting it back down onto his lap. He pauses for a moment, looking off in thought. He snaps out of the daze and looks back to the group. His eyes finally rest on Jeremy.

"They just kept coming. Waves and waves of 'em. We fought them off deep into that first night. It was unsettling at first. Killing them. But when we realized that it was kill or be killed, that primal instinct of survival kicked in. I remember the switch in myself.

There was a woman in our group who strayed out too far and was picked off by the pinks. I watched on as they relentlessly ripped her to pieces. They showed no remorse or concern. They only wanted to feed. And not even eat for necessity. They'd attack one person and move on to the next before they were even finished. They were never satisfied. Always wanting the next kill. That's when I switched to survival mode.

When their numbers began to finally dwindle, I tried again to reach my wife. No answer. I started to devise a plan on how to get to them. Her parents just lived across town. If I could just get out of the ports, I could get there and get them out of Savannah. As I was thinking about all this, my phone rang. It was my wife.

At first, all I could hear was static. Then her voice finally broke through. I could tell she was worried, her voice was tense. She began to ramble on and on about the news and everything that was going on. I kept trying to ask her if she and Emma were ok, but she just continued to babble on and on. I heard a loud banging in the background. Before I could even ask her what is was, she was telling me to hold on and that someone was at the door. I began yelling into the phone not to open it. Burton kept trying to quiet me down as my screaming was attracting more dead.

All I could hear was the screams of my wife over the phone. I could do nothing. The phone fell from my hand as I began to hear the screams of Emma. Mommy! Mommy! No! No!"

He stopped again. Tears poured from his face. His expression went blank as he began to wipe the tears from his eyes.

"I don't remember what happened in between then and now."

Tori looked over to Jeremy as the Lumberjack said this. Her face was one of concern. Jeremy noticed and turned his attention back to the broken man.

"What do you mean, you don't remember?" Jeremy asked.

The Lumberjack looked at him, his eyes bloodshot.

"I mean I don't remember. My mind has just blacked it out. Look, I told you what I remember. Can I go to sleep now?" He answered, his voice stern.

"Yeah man," Jeremy said. "Lexx, can you show him one of the offices where he can sleep?"

Lexx nodded and motioned for the Lumberjack to follow him down the hallway.

"Hey man, what's your name?" Ben asked.

"Andrew. But my friends all call me LJ."

"LJ?"

"Yeah, they all say I look like a lumberjack, so they call me LJ for short."

Lexx's mouth dropped open.

"All right LJ, get some rest," Jeremy said.

***

Once Lexx returned, the four of them gathered together in the storefront part of the building, away from the offices. They stood in silence for a moment before Jeremy finally spoke up.

"So, what do you guys think?"

"Well, the guy's a fighter for one. He's been out there since the beginning and he's still alive? That's amazing. And from what it sounds like, most of the time he's been alone" Ben said.

"That is what it sounded like," Tori pitched in. "What did you guys think about his story? Did everything seem ok to you?"

"What do you mean?" Lexx asked.

"Well, for starters, how about the fact that he doesn't even remember how he got here? If his story is correct, he clocked out somewhere last night. He doesn't remember what happened at all today? His memory just blocked out a whole entire day?"

"She does have a point," Jeremy adds. "I know that sometimes your brain will block out traumatic experiences. No doubt hearing your wife and daughter scream like that would be extremely traumatic, but I *saw* my mother get ripped apart and eaten and I have full memory of it. In fact, I can't forget it."

Jeremy tried to push the thoughts away as they began to creep back into his mind. He looked at the others. Out of the three of them, Tori looked the most concerned.

"Tori, what do you think?" Jeremy asked.

"I think," she started. "I think we should let him stay. For now. We could use an extra guy, especially one with an axe. Safety in numbers, right? I don't know. We should probably keep an eye on him though. He seems, um, unstable."

"Alright then, we let him stay. Any other concerns?"

Lexx and Ben both shook their heads.

"Good," Jeremy said. "Let's get some sleep. We've got a long day ahead of us, because tomorrow, we are going to get out of this city."

Chapter Twenty Four

Jeremy woke up to loud banging and yelling. He jumped to his feet as the others were stirring awake. He went out into the hall and ran down to the office that LJ was sleeping in. He wasn't there.

"What the hell is going on?" Tori said, walking up behind Jeremy. "Where's LJ?"

Jeremy shrugged.

"I'm guessing that's who's making all the noise."

He turned and looked at her. She held up her pistol, flipping the safety off. He nodded and turned to walk outside. They both walked through the warehouse out into the yard. Ben and Lexx, now awake, followed them outside.

There was LJ at the fence, shaking it, and yelling at the zombies beginning to surround it. Jeremy looked back at the others. They all had the same look on their face. The same look he had on his face. Concern.

"Hey! Hey you fuckers! Come here, you dead sons of bitches!"

As the dead got closer to the fence, LJ would take the pick end of his axe and push it through the chain link, hitting each one square in the forehead. With each one he let out a chuckle. Then he would yell again, attracting more corpses to the fence line.

"Hey, uh, LJ," Jeremy said, very nonchalantly. "Hey man, whatchu doin?"

The Lumberjack turned around to look at the group. He seemed surprised to see the four of them standing there, as if the noise he was making shouldn't have woken them up. He smiled and walked away from the fence.

"Just killing some of these zombies. Why? What's up? You guys ready to leave?"

"Almost. But you know that noise attracts these

things right? It's gonna be hard to leave when the streets are crawling with these z's," Jeremy answered.

"Yeah, I know noise attracts 'em. What do you think I'm yelling for? Just let me know when you're ready to clear out. I'll take care of this. Them."

He turned back to the fence and begins mumbling something to the zombies.

"You killed my wife. You killed my daughter. I'm going to kill every last one of you fuck-nuts."

Jeremy looked to the group and motioned for the four of them to retreat back inside. Lexx mouthed the word "cuckoo" and grinned. Once they were back inside, Jeremy closed the door and made sure LJ was still near the fence. He was.

"So, I think LJ may be cray-cray," he said.

"You think?" Tori said.

"Yeah, I'm starting to think that. Call it a hunch."

"Ok. So what do we do then?" Lexx asked.

"I don't know," Jeremy started. "The guy's been through a lot. I feel bad for him, I do. He has a reason to be pissed with the zombies and maybe he's just blowing off steam. An unconventional way of blowing off steam, but nonetheless, blowing off steam. Plus, he hasn't tried to harm any of us yet. I suggest we just keep an eye on him, but maybe he's gonna be alright?"

"Jer's got a point guys," Ben added.

"Yeah, but we just don't know this guy. What if he was psycho before all this went down? I mean, he seems to barely know himself," Tori said.

"So what do you suggest we do with him then, Tori?" Jeremy asked back.

She looked at Lexx for a moment as she thought about an answer. He nodded as if they were communicating telepathically again. She looked back at Jeremy.

"We leave him."

"No way," Ben interjected. "We can't just leave the

man! What if the Padre left Jeremy? Or hell, if Jeremy left me? Or if you and Lexx didn't join up? Out there, we are dead if we're on our own. If we leave him, we might as well just put a bullet in his head and I don't want that blood on my hands. I already have enough."

The end of Ben's sentence trailed off, everyone noticing and immediately realizing he was referring to leaving his grandmother in the hospital. Tori and Lexx share another look, knowing that if they want to make their case, they would have to tread lightly.

"Hey man, the guy survived out there on his own pretty all right so far," Lexx said, the calmest of the group.

"You saw how exhausted he was last night. He may have been able to last a couple of days on his own, but there is no way that he can do that forever," Ben said.

"Maybe he'll find another group of people. Maybe we're just not those people."

"This is crazy," Ben said, throwing up his hands. "We are talking about a man's life, aren't we?"

"We helped him out last night. Gave him a place to rest. Hell, he can stay here for all I care. I'm just saying, we don't owe him anything and he doesn't have to come with us," Tori said.

Ben shook his head.

"This is just wrong," he said.

"Wrong? Do 'right' and 'wrong' even have the same meaning anymore? He was right about one thing last night. Life is about survival now. Right and wrong are just ideals now," Lexx said.

"The world went to hell man; it doesn't mean that we shouldn't have morals anymore."

"Morals were a luxury. We just don't have that luxury anymore. It went out the window when dead people started eating people. It's survival of the fittest now. Well, it always was, it's just a lot more tangible now."

"Damn right."

The Lumberjack was standing in the doorway. Everyone looked surprised to see him there. He had snuck up on them without making a sound. He walked into the room, his head hung somewhat low.

"Hey, I'm sorry about this morning. I didn't mean to scare you guys. You probably think I'm crazy don't you?" he said.

"Hell yea-"

"We don't think you're crazy," Ben interrupted Tori, shooting her a dirty look. "We know you've been through a lot and we *all* understand that. But, are you gonna be okay?"

The question hung in the air for a moment, as Andrew pondered it. He knew what they meant. As soon as he saw them this morning outside, he knew that he had startled them with his freak out. He didn't even remember waking up and going outside. Just being there, seething in anger.

"Yeah, I think so," he finally answered. "I just hate those things so much. Took everything from me. Everything important."

Ben walked over to him and placed a hand on his shoulder. He seemed to appreciate it.

"Look, Andrew," Jeremy said. "You're welcome to join us get out of town, but do you think you can keep these episodes to a minimum?"

The man nodded.

"Good," Jeremy said, turning his attention to the warehouse. "There's an old delivery truck in the back of the warehouse. Let's round up what supplies we can out of here and fill it up. Then, we'll begin our trek west."

***

They all split up to scavenge what they could. Once

the others were gone, Tori pulled Jeremy aside. Her voice was firm but one of concern. Her body language on the other hand screamed that she was pissed. Her hands sat on her hips, which were cocked out to one side. She was biting her lip.

"Yes, Tori?"

"I don't think he should come along."

"You've made your concerns very clear. And I understand. I do. But I just think it's a bad idea leaving him here. It's just messed up. I can't imagine losing my wife, let alone a daughter. Give him some time."

"There's no time to mourn in this world."

"I know. And that's why we have to stick together."

She took a deep breath.

"Fine. But if he goes all banana sandwich again, that's on you."

She pushed him aside and walked off.

***

Once the truck was loaded, Jeremy gave LJ the signal to open the gate. Zombies were now wandering all over the street. Jeremy counted nine. Like a baseball player headed up to bat, LJ gave his axe a practice swing before revving up and bringing it down on the skull of a dead police officer. He knelt down and removed the still holstered Berretta. He waved his new find in the air before sticking into the back of his pants.

"Do you think someone should help him?" Tori asked from the passenger seat.

"First, you want to leave him and now you think he needs help? Make up your mind woman!" Jeremy said.

"I'm just saying..."

"He said he'd handle it since it was his fault they're here. Besides, Ben and Lexx are in the back ready to help him jump in the truck when we pull out of here."

The two men were holding onto handles in the back

of the box truck. Once Jeremy drove the truck out of the lot, LJ would jump in the back of the truck, they would close the door, and drive away. Simple plan. In theory.

"Holy shit!"

Jeremy snapped out of his daydream of everything working together smoothly to Tori's exclamation. LJ had reared back and Casey Jones'd a z's head right off her shoulders. The head went spinning through the air, mouth still snapping, and matted hair swirling. He turned with a smile and gave Jeremy the thumbs up. Jeremy put the truck in drive and pulled out onto the street. He watched as LJ jumped into the truck, via the side mirror, and heard the rolling door close in the back.

"He's in. Let's go," Tori said.

A smile formed on Jeremy's face as he drove away from the warehouse. For once, everything was going according to plan.

Chapter Twenty Five

Something was not right. Lexx was yelling from the back of the truck. The truck seemed to sway from side to side, as the men shuffled around in the box. Tori slammed her fist against the back of the cab.

"Hey! What's going on back there?" she yelled.

She looked at Jeremy and he nodded. He pulled the truck over into the parking lot of a grocery store. They got out and walked around to the back of the truck. Tori readied her pistol. Jeremy unlatched the door and flung it open. Ben and Lexx came running out of the truck. LJ was in the back corner, pistol raised.

"What the hell?" Tori asked.

"He's fuckin' bitten!" Lexx yelled.

"What?" She yelled back.

LJ put his pistol down and walked to the end of the truck. Lifting up his shirt, he revealed a badly infected bite wound right under his left ribcage. He grimaced and put his shirt back down. They all stood in silence for a minute. Jeremy thought about what to do. He knew from the movies that zombie bites were generally not good things. In the past few days however, he had not really seen anyone with just a bite. Every person he had seen attacked had been mauled in some way. No simple bites.

He looked at LJ's face. The man seemed a mix of worry and anger. He was probably worried on how the group would react to this unexpected announcement. And he was probably angry because he knew how they would most likely react.

"When did you get bitten?" Jeremy asked, breaking the silence, but not the tension.

"I don't know."

"Oh, that's convenient," Tori mumbled.

"Tori..." Jeremy said, giving her a firm look.

"Look, I don't know. It must have happened during my blackout. I swear I didn't know until it started to itch in the truck. I feel fine, just a little warm," LJ said.

He was sweating. The weather had cooled drastically from the day before. But that was November in Savannah for you. He might have a fever. Jeremy's mind began to race with possible outcomes.

"Everyone relax," Jeremy began. "We don't know much about what's going on, or this infection, or whatever it is. I think we all have seen zombie movies and know that this is not a good thing, but this whole thing hasn't played out just like the movies. He could recover from this. Maybe it's not the bite that kills you."

"We don't know that for sure," Tori said.

"You're right. The only thing we know for sure is that we don't know anything for sure."

She didn't seem to like that answer, but she did back down. Jeremy assumed that she would inform him of how she really felt once they were back in the cab of the truck. He looked forward to it.

"LJ, we'll keep an eye on your, your *condition*. If it gets to the point where we or you feel like you're going to turn into one of those things, we'll deal with it then. How would you-"

"Put a bullet in my brain before I turn into one of those things."

Jeremy was taken aback by the man's bluntness, but he understood. He didn't really want to be a citizen of the undead either.

"Ok then. For now, we continue on as normal."

Tori huffed when he said, 'normal,' but he ignored it. They were just outside of Rincon by a few miles and once they got that far, they still had a few more to go to Ben's parents. He looked over at the grocery store across the parking lot. He hated that the first thing he noticed was the scattered grocery carts. He hated it even more that it bothered him.

"While we're stopped here, let's check out that store and stock up on supplies. We can help supply Ben's parents in exchange for room and board. The store looks pretty abandoned," Jeremy said.

"There's a few z's over there by the dollar store," Lexx said, pointing to the opposite end of the strip mall.

There was a small group of them, three and a half as far as Jeremy could tell. The half being the upper torso of a middle aged man who crawled around on his hands. His bottom half was completely gone, except for the entrails that dragged behind him. They all wandered in front of the store aimlessly, bumping into each other and the building itself.

"We'll be sneaky-sneaky then," Jeremy said with a smile.

Lexx nodded and returned the smile.

***

Once inside the store, they decided it best to split up in pairs. Lexx and Tori wandered off towards the canned goods. Ben and Jeremy were going to try and see what the produce section looked like. The power was out in the building, but some of the fruits and vegetables should still be fresh. LJ went off on his own. Since the confrontation outside, he had not said much. Jeremy asked him if he was okay, to which he just nodded, and walked off.

Ben was also being really quiet. For having been so vocal in the argument over LJ earlier, he had been strangely silent since the parking lot. Once they got to the produce section, Jeremy decided to pick his brain a little bit.

"Hey man, you okay with LJ staying with us?"

Ben looked at him.

"Yeah. I'm cool with it."

"You sure? You've been kinda quite about the whole thing."

"I argued for him back at the warehouse didn't I? My opinion remains the same. It just bothers me how quick Tori and Lexx want to dump him."

He stopped before looking over some bananas and placing them into his cart.

"I get it, I do," he said. "I want to survive all this too. Trust me, I do. I already left my grandmother; I just can't leave someone behind like that again. I wasn't raised that way. My parents always taught me to do the right thing, you know, do unto others."

"I understand. Me too," Jeremy said. "My mom always had me in Sunday school. I got the being a good person talk many a time."

"Oh man, Sunday school. They didn't put this on the felt board did they?"

They both laughed. Jeremy picked up a tomato, but saw that the other side was starting to get mushy. He put it back down and moved down to the fruit. There were apples in bags that still looked fresh. He grabbed a couple of those and sat them in his cart. It almost felt like they were really shopping.

"Man, we went to this little old country church where the preacher was one of those fire and brimstone kinda guys," Ben said. "I still remember him preaching this scary as hell sermon on the rapture and the seven years of tribulation. I was so scared and didn't want to go through any of that, so I walked down the aisle and said the sinner's prayer. You ever do that?"

Jeremy nodded.

"Haha, yeah a couple times," he said.

"I did it every Sunday for a month straight. I wanted to make sure, you know?"

Ben paused for a second.

"You think any of that stuff was true? You think this is the end times?"

The question floored Jeremy. He had not really thought about it much. Everything going on lately, some of it did seem plausible. The church his mother went to didn't really teach a lot of stuff like that when he went. It was a lot more like don't drink alcohol or have sex outside of marriage. Basically, anything fun.

Could this be the end times though?

He thought about what the Padre told him about how this was not God's wrath, but maybe it was just our fault somehow. It made sense kinda. Maybe some scientist was trying to play god and wound up creating this disease? He remembered having to read Frankenstein back in high school. Could this whole thing be an experiment gone wrong? It all seemed so science fiction.

Jeremy still had a hard time accepting that God would just sit on the sidelines and watch though. His mother got up and read her Bible every day and went to church every Sunday she could. He didn't help her. Or the Padre, who apparently was someone who dedicated his life to the Lord's work.

Why isn't God doing anything? Where is He?

***

"Hold up, I need to get something from this aisle real quick."

Tori turned down the aisle before even really checking to see if Lexx was going to follow her or not. He quickly changed his direction.

"Are you getting what I think you're getting?" He asked.

"Yeah. Zombie apocalypse or not, a girl's still gonna need tampons," she said, as she reached up to grab a few boxes off the shelf. Lexx watched as she piled them into the cart.

"Geez, how many you takin'?"

"I don't know when we'll find more anytime soon, so I'd like to have a nice supply. Trust me, I can make these last."

Lexx started to look around as she placed a few more boxes in their cart. The "feminine hygiene" aisle was also the "family planning" aisle. Rows and rows of condoms, pregnancy tests, and assorted lubricants sat neighbor to the maxi-pads, and tampons.

Things kinda go full circle here, huh, he thought.

He picked up a pack of condoms off the shelf, turned it over, and began reading the back of the package. Tori eyed him with a smile creeping up on her face.

"You plan on using those anytime soon there, big boy?"

His face flushed red as he fumbled to put it back on the shelf.

"I uh, was just, uh, reading it," he said.

"Oh yeah? I bet that's some good reading there!"

"Shut up."

"You embarrassed, Lexington?"

He gave her a smile when she called him that.

"No, Victoria," he mocked. "Maybe I will grab some. I don't know when I'll be seeing them again, so I'd like to have a nice supply."

"Oh, haha. You are so funny. Good luck finding someone to use them with," she said as she walked away.

He wasn't sure if she was swaying her hips on purpose, or if it was just his imagination playing tricks on him. Could be both. The skin tight jeans she was wearing hugged her curves nicely and the oversized tourist t-shirt hung loose, exposing the bare skin of one of her shoulders.

He came up next to her and the cart, and emptied his arms of the thirty boxes he grabbed from the shelf. She let out a huge laugh. It was larger and louder than she expected, so she quickly covered her mouth. He chuckled at her awkwardness.

"Oh wow, someon"s full of themselves," she said.

"No, just confident. Besides, I've pretty much already been to second base with you. You wanna make it a grand slam?" he asked with a sly smirk.

"Uh, no. And going along with your stupid baseball analogy, whenever did we get to second base in your mind?"

"Downtown. You pretty much just flashed your breasts at me!"

She laughed at the way he said 'breasts.' This time she didn't hold back her giggles.

"That's not second base, you doofus! Second base is actually touching them! You, my friend, haven't even stepped up to bat yet!"

He stopped walking and put his hand on her waist. She immediately stopped and looked up at him. She fought against herself, but knew she was melting in his hands. He looked into her expectant green eyes and inched slowly closer to her face. She put up no fight as he leaned in and kissed her. Their lips locked for a few seconds, before he pulled away. She did not try to hide the big smile on her flushed red face.

"Not bad Lexington, not bad."

"You're not too shabby yourself, Victoria."

"And a gentleman too," she added. "You could have gone for more and I would have probably given it to you, but you didn't and I respect that."

He smiled and they continued to walk again. She started to say something else, but was cut off when the alarms went off. They looked at each other worriedly, grabbed the cart, and bolted for the front of the store.

***

"What the hell is going on?" Tori yelled, as they got

to the front of the store. "I thought the power was off?"

Ben and Jeremy got there the same time as Lexx and Tori. Jeremy threw up his hands in confusion. He winced as the alarm continued to blast throughout the store.

"Sometimes alarms are kept on a backup power source," Ben yelled. "Maybe this is one of those alarms?"

"Well, what the hell set it off then? We've been in this store too long for the alarm to just now be going off," she continued. "Wait. Where's LJ?"

Everyone else noticed that the fifth member of their group was still missing. Unlike the others, he had not run to the front of the store once the alarm started blaring. They began to look around to see if they could find him when there was loud crash from the pharmacy. They ran there and saw that it had been broken into and was the source of the alarm.

Jeremy walked in first cautiously. The others followed slowly and nearly bumped into a stopped Jeremy. There lying on the floor was an extremely intoxicated LJ covered in prescription pill bottles. He looked up to the group with a big, goofy smile and said,

"Hey guys! I feels better!"

Chapter Twenty Six

They stood there in disbelief as LJ struggled to get up to his feet. He was unsuccessful and fell back into the sea of orange bottles. He just laughed.

"You did this?" Tori screamed, drowning out the alarm. "You set off the alarm, you stupid son of a bitch? Fuck him! We are definitely leaving his ass now!"

She turned and glared at Jeremy. She was right. He nodded.

"We'll leave him. Just not here."

She started to protest, but he cut her off.

"Look, this place will be crawling with "s soon. We can't leave him here. We'll find him somewhere safe and leave him there."

"After all the trouble he's caused us?" she asked.

He only nodded, and proceeded to try and get the drunken man to his feet. His breath was hot with alcohol. He must have wandered off to the beer and wine aisle, before making his assault on the pharmacy. Ben and Lexx both joined Jeremy in helping the man up. Once they had him up, Ben started to put the small amount of fruit from their cart into Tori's.

"Here," he said. "Put him in the cart and we'll push him out of here."

Jeremy and Lexx moved LJ over to the cart and slowly lowered him into the basket. The man barely fit into it, his arm and legs dangling over the sides. He seemed to be having a hard time keeping his head up, because it swayed back and forth.

"You guys," he said between hiccups. "You guys are the best. Hiccup."

Ben moved a fuming Tori out of the way, taking control of the cart, and pushing towards the front of the store. They all ran, grabbing things off the shelves, and throwing them into the other cart. LJ began to laugh uncontrollably.

"Whee!" he yelled.

"Shut up!" Tori yelled through clenched teeth.

As they reached the storefront, Jeremy noticed that the parking lot's occupancy was much larger than when they entered the store. There were now several zombies wandering the parking lot. It was not until they got through the doors and got outside, that he realized how bad the situation actually was.

The parking lot was swarming with dead.

"Oh shit..."

The words slipped out of his mouth involuntarily. There was anywhere between fifty to seventy-five z's out there. He had yet to see that many of them group together like that. It was as if the pharmacy's alarm was the dinner bell and they were dinner. He noticed his mouth had also dropped open. He quickly closed it.

"We have to get out of here," he said quietly.

"No, you think?" Tori shot back.

"HEY GUYS! LOOK AT ALL THESE FUCKING ZOMBIES!"

Tori put her hand over LJ's mouth. He squirmed, so she put him in a sleeper hold.

"Nighty-night LJ."

He was out. Jeremy noticed that Lexx was trying to hide his smile. Even Jeremy had to admit, it was a cool trick. The truck was not far and most of the dead had not gotten that close to it yet. They pushed the carts to the truck and began loading the groceries into the back. Tori ran quickly up to the cab. She returned pumping a round into the shotgun. Once the men finished loading the groceries, they struggled to get LJ's dead weight into the back of the truck. He flopped onto the deck, letting out a moan, which was answered by other more-dead moans.

"Look out!"

Tori pushed Jeremy out of the way and blasted a

zombie that had wandered too close to the group. She took a huge chunk off the top of homeboy's head. His corpse fell with a thud. Ben and Lexx climbed into the truck and began closing the door.

"Thanks," Jeremy said.

"Don't mention it. Now get us out of here," she responded, as she pumped another round into the barrel.

Jeremy ran for the cab. The closest zombie was ten feet away. Too close for comfort. He left the keys in the ignition, just in case something bad happened and they had to bug out quickly. The truck roared to life. It was answered by more moans.

And then the shrieks came. Two of the runners, or pinkies, came sprinting full speed across the parking lot. They pushed and shoved their way through the crowd of grays, knocking over several of the less balanced zombies. Jeremy didn't give them much attention as he peeled out in the delivery truck. The truck fish-tailed, and both Lexx and Ben could be heard cursing in the rear.

He pulled the truck back out onto Highway 21 and headed west towards Rincon.

We'll be somewhere safe by the day's end.

This thought brought a smile to Jeremy's face. Ben told them that his parent's house was on a well, so they would have fresh water, and no shortage of it. They had plenty of generators and an old fuel tank full with reserves. They even had a chicken coop. He could almost taste the fresh omelets they'd be eating the next morning.

"What is that?"

Tori's question brought Jeremy back into reality. She was leaning forward and squinting, trying to make out something ahead of them. Jeremy began looking at the wide, dark shape that went from one side of the highway to the other. Something was blocking their way. It went all the way across the four-lane highway. As they got closer, a chill shot down Jeremy's spine as he slowly realized what the shape was.

It was a massive group of zombies.

A solid wall of rotting flesh stretched from one road shoulder to the other. As a group unit, they shambled towards the sound of the alarm. Which put the truck right between the two. Jeremy brought the truck to a stop.
"Turn around," Tori said slowly.
He put the truck in reverse and turned the truck in the opposite direction. Lexx was yelling, trying to figure out what was happening, but both Tori and Jeremy ignored him for the moment. Jeremy began driving back the way they came. He couldn't help but to continue to look in his side mirrors though. The dead were not moving quickly, but they were moving. It would only be a matter of time before they reached them if they did not get out of there.
They neared the store and the zombies there were wandering around the parking lot.
"What happened to the alarm?" Tori asked.
Jeremy listened. The alarm was off. The backup power source must have run out. He looked back in his mirror. The group was still steadily moving in their direction. It then dawned on Jeremy that the noise they were being attracted to was not the alarm. It was the truck.
This idea of his was confirmed when he realized that the dead in the parking lot were now also headed for the truck. He passed the grocery store.
"Where are you going?" Tori asked. "Back to Savannah?"
"Where else can I go? We've got z's coming from every direction!"

"Stop! Stop! Stop!" she yelled, pointing in front of them.

Another group of the undead, although not as large as the one from the west, was making their way towards them down Highway 21. Jeremy thought about weaving through them, but that would only lead them away from where they wanted to be. And right smack dab back where they didn't. So, he made a split decision.

He turned onto the entry ramp of southbound I-95.

"The interstate? Are you crazy?" Tori screamed.
"Not a lot of choices here."
"Man, this thing is gonna be packed, wall to wall cars!"
For once, Jeremy thought. *I hope she is wrong.*

***

She was. The southbound side of Interstate 95 was mostly clear. There were some abandoned cars and the occasional semi, but for the most part, pretty easy to navigate. The northbound side, on the other hand, was not so lucky.

Traffic filled all three lanes. It seemed to go on for as far as Jeremy could see. The cars were all passengerless except where the passengers were unable to leave. There were quite a few zombies still strapped in by their seat belts. Blood covered the inside of windows where someone must have turned inside their vehicle. Or where family members were forced to put down one of their loved ones.

He looked over at Tori. She did not seem to be too upset that she was wrong. Her eyes went from car to car on the northbound side. She scanned for any threat lurking amongst the graveyard of vehicles. Jeremy decided to ride in silence and save talking about what they were going to do with LJ for later. For now, he'll just focus on how to get to Rincon from 95. He wasn't too familiar with the area. Jeremy rarely came out this far west. Downtown was normally as west as he got. Hopefully, Ben would know how to get to his parents from here.

There was a banging on the wall separating the cab from the back.

"Hey guys, you might want to pull over when you get a chance," Lexx said through the wall.

Jeremy looked at Tori.

"It's clear. We can stop here. I'll keep an eye out, while you go see what's going on," she said.

He nodded, and brought the truck to a stop. He grabbed LJ's pistol from the console and walked to the back of the truck. His mind raced with ideas of what could be wrong. Was LJ turning? Did he already turn and now Jeremy had to finish him off? His hand gripped the pistol tight as he knocked on the back door.

It slid open to reveal Lexx and a crouching Ben. Ben was kneeling next to LJ; his hand on the man's sweating forehead. Jeremy relaxed. He wasn't really ready for a mercy killing yet. Killing zombies was one thing, but putting someone off so they don't turn into a zombie? That still feels too much like murder.

"What's up?" Jeremy asked, as casual as he could muster.

"His fever's getting worse. Ridin' in the back of a truck ain't helping either," Lexx said. He looked back at the man, who was still out cold, but breathing heavily. His breaths were strained and wheezy. He didn't look good. He looked like death.

"Look, I hate to say it, but if we're gonna need to stop somewhere, we need to do it soon," he continued. "I don't think it would be right to leave him, even though he did screw us over big time. I'll handle talking to Tori about it. You just find us somewhere to go. And quick."

Lexx turned and looked back at LJ again and then back to Jeremy. The change of heart in Lexx surprised Jeremy. Maybe Lexx was right about himself and there really was more to him than his gruff exterior. Jeremy was also sure that riding in the back with Ben had something to do with it too. Or perhaps seeing the dying man.

They were near the exit ramp to Highway 80. Pooler, a suburb of Savannah, was right there off the exit. There should be somewhere they could go there. Jeremy ran his hand through his hair, searching his brain for somewhere that would be safe. He went to walk back to the cab, but stopped. That's it. The answer to where they would stay was right in front of him.

On the other side of the congested northbound lane, down a small slope, and past some small ponds, was a huge building with a glass front. The whole front must have been windows. Backhoes and front loaders in striking poses were dotted across the landscape. It was one of the largest construction vehicle manufacturers in the world. And now, it was gonna be the place where they spent the night.

Chapter Twenty Seven

For having been so hot the other day, there was a cold chill in the air as they pulled the truck up to the building's loading docks. Jeremy backed it up like a pro to which he received a nod of approval from Tori. They got out and walked over to the stairs that led up to the loading dock. The truck's bed was now level with the dock, so the men in the back of the truck would be able to easily walk right out. Jeremy lifted the door and they did just that.

"What do we do with him?" Tori asked, pointing her thumb at LJ.

"He should be safe here," Jeremy said. "We'll just close the door. This loading area is pretty tucked in here."

The building was only accessible by a road that turned off of Highway 80 and had a series of check points that you would normally have to pass through. But being that it was the zombie apocalypse and all, they had no trouble getting through said check points. The gates were all broken, but broken *out* and not *in*. People were trying to leave this place, not get in.

This thought comforted Jeremy, because he was not ready to deal with anymore survivors. Granted, the hipsters downtown were probably a little crazier than your normal survivor. Still, Jeremy really had no desire to fight over territory, or supplies, of which they had little. Due to the Lumberjack's raid of the pharmacy, their shopping trip turned out to be a big bust. They had some fresh fruit, snack foods, a few bottled drinks, tampons and more condoms than anyone should ever really need or use.

"Alright, grab your guns and let's give this place a look over," Jeremy said as he held up LJ's pistol.

Lexx handed Ben the rifle.

"Here man, you're probably the better shot."

"Probably?" Ben asked with a smirk.

"Ok, ok. You're the better shot. But I'd like to see you jump from a second story balcony and shank somebody."

The two men chuckled.

"Hey, when you guys are done jerking each other off, can we get started already?"

Tori stood at the door into the building, tapping her foot. She had the shotgun propped up on her shoulder. She looked business.

"Jeez, babe," Lexx said. "What's the hurry?"

"The hurry, *babe*, is that it will be dark soon, we're not at Ben's parents yet, and we have an infected asshole in the back of that truck with all our food and supplies."

He walked up to her and grinned.

"Point made. After you."

He held out his hand for her to walk in. She huffed and swung open the door. The lights detected motion and flickered to life. Jeremy closed the truck's door and followed everyone else inside.

***

The place was a maze at first. Hallways twisting and turning throughout the building. There were a lot of offices and work areas filled with cubicles. So far, it only looked like a business, not a manufacturer of construction equipment.

That was until they entered the main foyer. Two, bright yellow machines graced the showroom's floor on either side of the room. A massive, spiraling staircase wound up to the second floor, where there was a balcony and what looked like more offices. A walkway crossed over to a platform on the front side of the building. The whole front wall was windows like

Jeremy thought. The windows were tinted on the outside though, keeping the sun from blaring through. The room was cool too, so it must help with the heat as well. He would not be surprised if they were double-paned.

Good. A zombie wouldn't be able to break through that.

A lone desk sat in the middle of the room. Probably to greet visitors and the higher-ups visiting the building. They walked over to it. Jeremy leaned over the desk to get a look behind it and gasped.

"What?" Lexx asked.

Jeremy shook his head and walked around to the other side of the desk. They followed him and stopped. Tori put her hand up to her mouth and Ben looked away.

On the ground lay half of the front desk secretary. Her legs were completely gone, her tailbone hanging out of the bottom of her torso. Intestines hung from the open cavity. Her blouse was torn open. She groaned and held up a hand reaching for Jeremy. She was still alive.

"I got it," Tori said.

She came up to the dead woman and brought the butt end of the shotgun down onto her head. There was a sickening crunch as wood and bone collided. It wasn't the crunch that got to Jeremy, but the slosh of brain matter afterwards. He threw up.

"You ok?" Tori asked, once he finished.

He nodded. He had seen a lot of gore and gross things the past few days, and maybe it was finally just catching up to him. It was about time he hurled. The only downside was now he was hungry. He tried not to think about it too much. The thought of food was making him feel a little queasy.

It was then he noticed a sign with arrows on it. One arrow pointed to the left and said, "AUDITORIUM" and the other arrow pointed right with the word, "ASSEMBLY" underneath it. Jeremy looked at the others

"Auditorium or assembly?" he asked.

The consensus was auditorium first, assembly on the way back to the truck. They walked to the left of the sign and entered a long hallway. One side was all glass windows, the same as the foyer, and the other wall was filled with pictures telling the history of the company. An old black and white photo of a few men standing next to a tractor caught Jeremy's eye. They stood there proudly with their workmanship.

Auditorium was an understatement. More like full-fledged theater. A huge projection screen, a stage and rows and rows of cushioned, reclining seats filled the room. There was even a soda fountain. With Coke.

"Oh man, is that Coke?" Lexx said, running over to the machine. He grabbed a cup from the dispenser and put it under the fountain head. Taking a deep breath first, he then pressed the button. Cold, brown liquid began to fill the cup. He began to jump up and down.

"It works! It works! I'm sleeping in here for sure!" he yelled.

The others laughed and went to join him. After finishing their drinks in silence, Jeremy decided to bring up LJ and what they should do with him.

"I've been thinking about LJ and I don't think he has much longer," he said. "I know I said after what he did, we would find somewhere safe and leave him, but I don't think we should do that anymore. I doubt he'll make it through tomorrow, maybe even tonight. I say we just wait for him to turn, put him out of his misery and then make the rest of our journey to Ben's house."

He paused waiting for Tori's rebuttal. She said nothing. They locked eyes, but still nothing.

"Tori, you ok with that?" Jeremy asked.

"Yes. If you think that's what we should do, than

yes. I may have overreacted back at the store. We can wait for him to turn."

She looked over to Lexx and he nodded. Jeremy began to wonder if Lexx had anything to do with her change of heart. The two seemed closer since the grocery store, but Jeremy had not thought to ask about it yet.

"Good. Any other concerns?" he asked.

Nobody said anything. They were all exhausted. The only concern now was sleep.

"Well, I say we set up camp in here. Those padded seats are looking really comfy right about now, or maybe it's the fact that we slept in warehouses the past two nights," Jeremy said.

Everyone chuckled. They were tired, but their spirits were high. They had a safe place for the night and tomorrow they would get out of the city. Things would be good tomorrow. Jeremy started thinking about the fresh eggs again.

Soon.

They eventually made their way back out to the truck. Passing through the assembly area, they learned that they could cut through directly to the loading dock, bypassing all the offices. It was a huge, open room with giant ceiling fans. The blades had to be at least ten feet long each. It was the biggest fan Jeremy had ever seen. There were many workbenches that had a lot of hand tools and a few power tools were spotted over in a metal cage.

They brought LJ inside and set him up in one of the offices. Lexx handed him a cup of Coke to drink. He was awake, but his fever continued to spike and he was overheating. Lexx left and came back with several cups of ice to help cool the man down. Once they got LJ situated, they informed him that they would come back and check on him before they called it a night and then again in the morning.

He muttered something about his wife and daughter, then passed out from the exhaustion. The group closed the door behind them when they left and headed back towards the auditorium. They picked up several hand tools while passing through the assembly area, just in case they found anymore straggler z's and they needed to take them out quietly.

***

Tori leaned back in her chair, stretching out like a cat. She let off a big yawn, which set off a chain reaction of yawning.

"Sorry guys," she said. "I guess I'm more tired than I thought."

"It's okay Tori, I think we're all tired," Ben said.

He was munching on some fruit snacks that made the trip from the grocery store. His feet were propped up on the chair in front of him. He was tossing the tiny snacks into the air and catching them in his mouth. The others would applaud when he was successful.

Lexx got up from his seat to go over and fix another cup of Coke. When he sat back down, he had a grin on his face.

"What's so funny?" Tori asked.

"Oh, it's nothing. I just love Coke," he said.

He sat back down and started sipping his drink. Jeremy was happy that they found somewhere safe for the night. As much as he wished they were already at Ben's place, this was a great secondary option. There was still power here. The plant must be on its own power grid. They had Coke. Which was more important to some than others. And they actually had something comfy to sleep on. Not a makeshift bed on a shelf or a crummy office chair and desk. The theater chairs' cushions were still plump. They weren't worn down with overuse like the ones in a normal movie theater.

These seats probably don't get much action.

"I guess we won't find out what happened to LJ that day he has no memory of."

Ben broke the peaceful quiet.

"Not that we would, he didn't even remember," Tori said.

"Yeah, I know. Maybe he would though. Sorry, I was just thinking out loud."

"It's cool man," said Lexx. "Speaking of the Lumberjack, should we go check on him? I'm getting pretty tired, so I'd like to turn in soon. Screw it. I'll go check on him."

"Yeah, that'd be great," Jeremy answered.

"Don't look at me. I'm about to fall asleep over here," Ben added.

Lexx tuned his gaze to Tori. She looked up from her own comfortable spot and shook her head no.

"Do not ask me to leave this very, very comfy spot."

"Tori, you want to come with me?" he asked.

She let out a groan.

"Ugh. Ok, ok..."

He smiled as she stood up and they walked out together. Ben sat up for a second and looked over at Jeremy.

"They together?" he mouthed.

"Yeah, I think so," Jeremy said.

Ben smiled and drifted off to sleep. Jeremy reached for his bag and pulled his Mother's Bible out of his bag. He flipped through the pages, which were covered in handwritten notes. The thought of maybe finding some help in this thing was soon overpowered by the sight of his mother's handwriting. He placed the book back in the bag.

I'll go through that later, he thought.

Her death was still too fresh in his mind. He promised himself that he would read it, just not yet. The Padre's journal caught his eye. Maybe he could find something encouraging in it. Something to give him hope. He pulled out the leather-bound book and began to read.

***

March 31st, 2011
It has been thirty days since my last contact with the Church. They have ceased all communication with me and according to the priests in the nearby towns, with them as well. I am not sure what is going on. I will continue to shepherd my small flock until I hear from the diocese.

September 13th, 2011
It has now been six months since my last entry and seven months since contact with the Church. The other priests and myself are concerned with the absence of communication with Rome. Our Bishop is missing and I am hearing the rumor that all Bishops of México are missing. Only the local priests are remaining. It seems that the Church has abandoned México all together.

I have arranged to meet with some of the other priests to study the scriptures. As of right now, it is all we have. We will continue to administer the sacraments to our flocks and read from the Holy Scriptures. Praying that we will hear from the Church.

April 4th, 2012
It has now been over a year since contact with anyone outside of México. The other priests and I have given up on hearing anything from Rome. Our flocks have remained faithful, and some, including my own, have actually grown.

In accordance with the scriptures, we have cut back on

some of the sacraments, finding them, unnecessary. The Lord's Table and Baptism have remained staples, as we see them administered in the scriptures. The changes we have made are radical, but Rome has abandoned us, and the scriptures are all we have. They are now our authority.

Not all priests are happy with these changes. They accuse us of dividing the Church and say that we are acting like the reformers of old. Maybe it has something to do with the two Baptist missionaries from the States.

They have been here in the village for several months now, working construction, and helping the locals. At night time, they hold Bible studies and teach the people about the Lord Jesus. I cannot complain as it is bringing the people back into the church. Their house meetings have grown so large that I have allowed them to use the church building for their bible studies.

I must admit, that even I have taken many notes from them. Their knowledge of the word is extensive, even more extensive than my own church training. They have recommended and gifted books to me by men named Piper and MacArthur. MacArthur's commentaries on the New Testament have proved to be invaluable in my teaching Mass. Piper's are weighty, and at times, it seems that there are more footnotes than actual writing. But they are still ripe with information.

I feel as if the Father has sent these two missionaries here to us. May He be praised. When Rome abandoned us, the Father did not.

August 13th, 2012
Our two friends are leaving tomorrow to head back to their home in the States. It has been a great blessing having them here with us. The people and I are greatly excited to get to work in spreading the Gospel throughout México. A true revival has happened here and in the neighboring villages.

Travis and Daniel, who the locals have taken to calling 'Paul and Barnabas', have invited me to come visit them in their hometown of Savannah, Georgia sometime, and to be a missionary there. Ha! Me? A missionary to the United States? I asked them if that was even needed and they said, "Yes. Sadly so."

Maybe. Maybe one day I will journey to America.

November 3rd, 2012
My bags are packed and I am ready to head north to Savannah, Georgia! Since our missionary friends have left, I have had many men step up in the church who are helping me lead our ever growing flock. I am confident in them that they will take care of things while I am gone.

I am lucky to have been practicing my English for so long, that hopefully I will not need a translator! The journey will be long and it will take me a few weeks to reach my destination, but by God's grace, I will get there!

***

Jeremy closed the journal after reading the last entry. His mind raced with the Padre's story. How the church abandoned him and how God provided two missionaries to fill the hole. Some of what the Padre said seemed to make more sense now. That God knew what he was doing, even when it seemed like he was not there. Jeremy didn't feel the comfort like he wanted, but he did feel a peace about things. Not that things were great, but that maybe everything would eventually be okay. Maybe they would be alright. The thoughts continued to swirl around in his head until he felt his eyes begin to grow heavy and soon he was fast asleep.

***

It was not long into their journey before Tori had Lexx pressed up against the wall. She was definitely the more aggressive one, which she liked. The fact that he wasn't pushing her, made her only want him more. Even when her hand would move a little too far south, he would grab it firmly, and place it back on his chest. These small gestures only seemed to fuel her fire.

"Hey, hey" Lexx said, pushing her back so he could get some oxygen. "Let's slow down just a little."

"Said no guy ever," she responded somewhat annoyed.

"I said just a little."

His hand slid down her back, ending with him grabbing a cheekful. She went back to push him against the wall, but he sidestepped her.

"For real though," he continued. "Let's at least go check on LJ first."

"I do not get you Lexx," she said as she began to walk away from him down the hall. "Here I am practically throwing myself on you and you want to take it slow."

"And I appreciate that Victoria, but I would rather go check on the man first, and then give you my undivided attention. Plus, I'm enjoying the anticipation that's building up here between us."

"Are you stringing me along, Lexington?"

"Maybe," he said with a coy smile.

"You rat bastard."

She playfully punched him in the arm.

Fine, she thought. *If that's the game he wants to play, then two can play that game.*

She walked away, slightly shaking her hips as she went. She knew he was watching her because he lingered a minute before catching up to her.

When they got to the office where LJ was staying, they paused for a moment at the door. LJ could be heard through the door mumbling to himself. Lexx leaned in to try and get a better listen, but he shook his head. He couldn't make out what the man was saying.

"Here we go," Lexx said as he reached for the door handle.

LJ was tucked into the corner of the room, asleep in the fetal position. He was drenched in sweat and shivering. The fever must have grown worse since they left him. The shivering was borderline convulsions. He had been talking in his sleep and his mumbling was much more intelligible now.

"Killed them. Killed them all. I did it. I did it. I killed them all."

Tori looked at Lexx.

"He must be talking about the zombies at the port," Lexx said.

Tori nodded as she leaned in to feel the man's forehead. It was burning up, but slick with perspiration. She wiped her hand on the back of Lexx's leg. He turned and gave her a disgusted look. She giggled. This caused LJ to stir and turn over to his other side, so he was facing away from them.

"Alright, let's go. There's not much we can do for him. We'll come back and check on him in the morning," Tori said, standing up.

Lexx nodded and they retreated to the doorway. LJ began to mumble again. They stopped to listen to the man sleep talk.

"I did it. I did it. Killed them. Killed Burton. Killed the girls. Killed everyone. I did it. I did it."

Horror crept up on their faces as LJ began to rant about having killed his friend and everyone there with him at the port. The man went on for a few moments before finally relaxing and falling into a deep sleep. Tori grabbed Lexx by the arm and pulled him outside. She closed the door and pushed a nearby large trash can in front of it.

"What. The. Fuck," she said. "That's what happened? He killed everyone? That's what he doesn't remember? How do you forget that?"

Lexx shook his head. He was trying to wrap his head around the situation.

"I knew this guy was bad news. I fucking knew it," she continued. "We gotta go tell Jeremy and Ben."

"Hold on," Lexx finally said. "We'll tell them in the morning. He's not going anywhere and he's not much of a threat now. You saw him. The guy's on the verge of death. We'll deal with it tomorrow."

She seemed hesitant to his response, but he watched as it slowly sunk in. She nodded. She didn't like it, but she nodded. She knew Lexx had a point. The guy was not going anywhere. And the important thing was: She was right.

"How do you just block killing everyone around you from your memory though?" she asked as they walked back to the theater.

"He must have freaked out when he got the call from his wife. What did Jeremy call it, "the rage?" Maybe that's what happened."

He shrugged. She knew that Jeremy had mentioned the whole "rage" thing, but she didn't know what to think of it. She hadn't experienced it, neither had Ben or Lexx. Maybe it only happens in time of extreme grief. She just didn't know. And she did not like that.

When they reached the theater, they decided they didn't really feel much like fooling around after that. They picked out seats close to each other and got comfortable. Both Ben and Jeremy were long gone to slumber-land. Tori began to close her eyes and drift away, when she felt something touch her hand. It was Lexx. He set his hand down on top of hers and they both fell asleep.

Chapter Twenty Eight

Ben opened his eyes. He'd grown accustomed to waking up in strange places the past few days, so the fact that he was in a theater didn't alarm him at all. He sat up and stretched his arms toward the ceiling. The theater chairs were the comfiest thing he'd slept on recently, but they still left him a little stiff and sore. He missed his bed. He'd even settle for his old, twin-sized bed at his parent's house. Hopefully, he'd be sleeping in that by tonight.

No one else was awake yet. He didn't even remember Lexx and Tori coming back in last night. The last thing he remembered was asking Jeremy if they were together. He smiled at the thought of those two hitting it off. With everything that was going on in the world right now, it was nice to know that people can still fall in love. It gave Ben hope.

He quietly got up from his seat and made his way to the Coke machine. He winced at the noise of it loudly sloshing into the cup. It was a little louder than he expected. Or maybe because it was so quiet, that only made it seem louder. He filled the cup and took a sip. Delicious.

Ben decided to go check on LJ while the others slept in. They needed their rest. Ben on the other hand knew that he didn't need much sleep to recharge. Four-six hours at the most. Any more than that and he'd be groggy. His sleep patterns were probably developed during his college days and set in stone when he started working for "The Lady." Being her social media manager was a lot harder than what some might think. She could be quite demanding on when she wanted her tweets and posts to go out. A lot of the locals didn't care for her, but Ben admired her. She made herself from nothing into something. You have to give her credit for that.

As he walked down the hallways of the massive building, he wondered what the place was like before the dead started coming back to life. Would it have been bustling with workers and office drones right now? Were they busy this time of year or slow? He wiped sleep from his eyes as he turned the corner to the hallway where LJ was located. He stopped dead in his tracks.

The door was missing from its hinges. Missing was an understatement. It looked like it had been ripped off. There was still wood from the door attached to the hinges, but the door was sitting out in the hallway.

This is not good, Ben thought.

He ran up to the door and held his hand up to his mouth in shock. The room was soaked in blood. A huge puddle of fresh, crimson blood covered the floor, and handprints were all over the walls, like an early cave mural. Footprints led away from the puddle and out into the hallway. LJ, or what might be left of him, was nowhere to be found.

"Oh shit," Ben muttered, fear beginning to surge throughout his bloodstream.

He had to go wake the others and tell them. To warn them. He turned and ran back the way he came. His mind was racing.

Did the zombies get in? Did they eat LJ? Did he turn into one of them?

The thoughts kept jumping into his mind. Then, he heard the roar.

It wasn't a moan. And it wasn't like the runners' shrieks. It was a thundering, booming roar. A scary-as-hell roar. It came from somewhere in the building, but Ben couldn't pinpoint it, because it seemed to bounce off all of the walls.

"Oh shit, oh shit, oh shit," he began to repeat over and over to himself.

Could it be something new? First the zombies, and then the runners, and now something new? Ben shivered at the thought. The crazy runners were bad enough. Hell, they haven't even really fought any of those! They always ran from them! If there's something worse than those...

Ben ran like hell.

He came flying around the corner into the main foyer area.
Almost there, he thought.

And there it was.

"It" being the thing that made the horrible sound. It was huge. Seven-eight feet tall, massive build, grotesque muscles that burst through the skin upon rapid growth. The skin hung off its giant frame like loose clothing. The muscles themselves seemed to be pulsating. Possibly even still growing. Its left shoulder almost looked like it had a gangrenous tumor growing from within it, but it was all grotesque muscle. The thing's neck was probably as think as Ben's waist. It stood there like a 'roided-out monument to all that was evil.
But then Ben realized something. Something he wished he hadn't realized. This was no new creature. It wasn't some evolution of the dead infection or even some demon from the darkest parts of the abyss. Ben shuddered, his stomach muscles tightening.

It was LJ.

The man must have turned during the night and when he did, he turned into something really, really nasty. The infection, or whatever it was that is doing all this, must have affected him differently somehow, causing the man to mutate into this monster.

Monster.

The word echoed in Ben's head. Ben began to back away slowly from the infected LJ, but the thing had already locked its dead, lifeless eyes on him. It let out a deafening bellow. Ben was unarmed and he cursed himself for not grabbing something. Anything. He took off running for the auditorium.

He ran as fast as he could, but could feel the beast gaining behind him. With each step the thing took, the floor shook. Ben never turned to see how close it was getting. He could smell it getting closer.

"Guys! Guys! Wake up!" Ben yelled.

And the next thing he knew, he was flying through the air. It had picked Ben off the ground and thrown him back in the direction of the main entrance. He hit the ground with tremendous force. He was sure that he cracked a rib. Wincing at the pain, he tried to get to his feet, but the thing was already back on top of him.

It began to pummel him, over and over, with its giant fists. He tried to hold his hands up to deflect the blows, but his arms snapped against the pressure. It seemed to have no desire to eat Ben. It only wanted to kill him. To destroy him. And it was succeeding.

His vision began to go blurry, but at this point, he didn't really care. He just wanted it to be over. This was it for him. He just hoped the others were able to get away. He hoped his shouting was enough warning. The monster lifted him up by the leg, staring into Ben's face with its black, evil eyes and then tore the man in two, splitting him at the waist.

***

Jeremy snapped awake when he heard Ben's yelling. Something was wrong. He jumped up out of his seat and grabbed the Beretta from his bag. Tori and Lexx were right behind him, each armed with the rifle and shotgun, respectively.

"It sounded like it came from the hall," Jeremy yelled, as he ran towards the hallway.

There was no one there. He continued moving down the hall.

Maybe Ben was running away from something, he thought.

There could be z's in the building and Ben had to get away quick. He yelled to warn them. Jeremy ran into the main room and came to an abrupt stop.

"No!" he yelled.

There was Ben. What was left of him. Pieces of his body lay in a bloody pool of carnage. Something had torn Ben limb from limb. Jeremy couldn't believe it.

"No, no, no," he cried. "Ben... no..."

The others came up behind him and put their hands on his shoulders, to try and hold him steady. Jeremy fell to his knees and just stared into the mess of what was once Ben. He felt anger began to surge through his veins again. The rage was building. His body trembled, and his fists clenched, as the adrenaline skyrocketed throughout him.

"What did this?" he asked. "There aren't even any bite marks."

Tori looked at Lexx.

"It must have been LJ," she said.

"LJ? A zombie wouldn't do this. A zombie would still be here, eating him."

"We think LJ had some issues."

"What do you mean?" he asked, turning to look at the couple. His face was red.

"We overheard him talking in his sleep. He was talking about how he killed everyone that was with him at the ports, even his friend. That's why he doesn't remember, because he got the rage and killed everyone," she said calmly.

When Jeremy heard her say something about the rage, he tried to calm himself down. He wouldn't lose control of himself like LJ had. He wouldn't kill his friends. But, he might kill LJ.

"But why this with Ben?" Jeremy asked, confused why it only killed Ben and did not eat him.

"Maybe the combination of the rage and the infection made him something worse, man," Lexx said. He knelt down to Jeremy's eye level. The look on his face was one of sympathy and concern.

"We need to get going now, Jeremy. There's nothing we can do for Ben," Tori said. She looked around, making sure the coast was still clear. Jeremy nodded, but he couldn't feel the strength in his legs to stand up yet.

"Ben was a good man. For the short time I knew him, I'm glad I did," she added. "But there is nothing we can do-"

She was interrupted when they heard a faint moan. Their heads all turned slowly and looked towards the source of the moan.

It was Ben.

His head moved around, jaws slowly snapping up and down. His graying eyes caught sight of the group and it began to try and move towards them. Only the head moved. It seemed agitated that it was not getting nearer to its food. Jeremy stood up and wiped the tears from his eyes.

"There is one last thing we can do for him," he said.

Jeremy pointed the pistol's barrel at what was once his friend Ben's head and pulled the trigger. The gunshot was answered by a roar in the distance.

Chapter Twenty Nine

"We need to leave! Now!" Tori demanded.

They ran for the auditorium.

"Let's just grab what we can and get to the truck," she yelled as they entered the room. "Lexx, leave the Coke!"

"Aww, mom!" he mock-whined as he began to stuff food back into bags.

Jeremy fumbled with his bag, trying to get the Padre's journal back into it. He remembered reading it the night before, but must have fallen asleep reading it. Right now, he was focused on getting his bag packed.

He couldn't believe Ben was gone. He'd only known the guy a few days, but they really bonded over them. Fighting for your life with someone will do that to you. He didn't even know his last name. It was then that he realized that they were heading to Ben's parents. They had no idea how to get there. Ben was going to switch spots with Tori once they got closer and explain how to get there. Now he was gone. They now had nowhere to go.

Jeremy immediately felt guilty for even thinking about it like that. Ben was dead. If his parents were still alive, they had no way to know their son was dead. Jeremy tried not to think about that and just focused on getting everything together.

"Y'all ready?" Lexx asked.

"I am," Tori said. "Jeremy, you gonna make it?"

He nodded.

"Yeah, let's go," he finally said.

They ran back out into the hallway. Jeremy looked out the windows to the right. The area between the building and interstate was now covered with zombies.

"Oh no," he said, stopping mid-run to stare out the window.

"What?" Tori yelled before stopping herself and looking.

The three of them stood there and watched as what looked like hundreds of zombies shambled across the landscape. The massive group they saw the day before must have followed them here. They took a long time, but they got there and now Jeremy and the others were completely surrounded. They might have a shot if they were able to get to the truck.

"C'mon, let's go!" Tori said, tugging on Jeremy's sleeve.

They began running again. Jeremy's bag slapped up and down on his back. He held two pistols in his hands. He knew one had half a clip, the other was only missing one bullet. He thought about the other ammo. Lexx's shotgun had three shells and Tori's rifle had maybe five rounds left in it. Maybe four. Everything else was still in the truck.

As they entered the main foyer area, they heard a roar again. This time much, much closer. Looking up they saw what was once LJ standing on the balcony of the second floor. Its dark, blackened eyes fell on them. It snarled again and then jumped from the balcony. It landed on its feet, putting deep fissures into the floor.

"Die, you son of a bitch!" Jeremy yelled as he began unloading one of the pistols into the monster. The bullets hit in the chest first, but slowly rose upwards as Jeremy readjusted his aim. The last round in the clip hit the thing right square in the forehead. Its head flew back.

But it didn't die. Blood oozed from the wound, but the beast seems unfazed. It bellowed, or laughed possibly, and lunged for Jeremy.

"I shot it in the fucking head!" he yelled, as the thing came at him.

Boom.

Lexx blasted the thing dead on with the shotgun, sending the creature sprawling. He looked at Tori and then to Jeremy.

"Jeremy, get her out of here," he said.

Jeremy looked at the man dumbfounded. Tori began to protest, but he pulled her in quickly and planted one right on her lips.

"Victoria, I really did want to bone the shit out of you," he said with a coy smile before pushing her back into Jeremy's direction. The infected Lumberjack was getting back up and rearing to attack.

"Jeremy, now!"

Jeremy grabbed Tori by the wrist and pulled her away from Lexx and towards the truck. Lexx pumped another round into the shotgun.

"C'mon big boy! Come and get it!"

Jeremy didn't look back to see what happened, but could barely make out the shotgun blast over the sound of his own beating heart.

***

Jeremy's mind shifted into "shit-storm survival mode." He was still having to pull Tori by the wrist. She was no longer resisting, but she wasn't really willfully following him. Her eyes were glazed over. He felt bad for her, he did, but he had to get her out of here. For Lexx.

He kicked open the door to the loading dock. They ran outside, but quickly about-faced. The loading dock area was being swarmed by the dead.

"Shit!" Jeremy cursed.

His cursing brought the unwanted attention of the dead and they began their shambling towards him and Tori. He pushed her back through the door and slammed it shut.

What to do?

The truck was surrounded. The front was covered with z's and Lexx was fighting LJ to the death in the foyer.

Where were they going to go?

His thoughts were interrupted when a group of z's came around a hallway corner.

They were in the building too? Not good. Not good.

Jeremy grabbed Tori and pulled her in the opposite direction of the oncoming zombies.

"Tori! I need you to snap out of it! We have to get out of here!"

She seemed to acknowledge his words, but they didn't sink in. She remained lost in her own thoughts. He continued to pull her along until they finally lost their zombie tail. There was a door marked, "Custodial Office." He opened the door and pushed her inside. He quickly closed the door, locking it just as fast. He pushed a heavy file cabinet in front of the door, just to be on the safe side. Collapsing against the wall and onto the floor, Jeremy thought about how epically fucked they were.

***

Lexx didn't have time to see if they got to safety or not. The beast lunged at him as Jeremy and Tori ran away. He blasted it again with the shotgun, but the buckshot only grazed the thing this time. It was able to still strike Lexx, bringing its clawed fist across his shoulder. The pain was immense, but Lexx was able to keep himself together.

One shell left.

He had to do something.

If he could just lure it into the assembly area, there had to be something there that could kill this thing. He brought the butt end of the gun across the thing's face. It grimaced, but didn't seem too fazed by the blow.

Duh, Lexx. If it got shot in the FACE and walked it off, I'm pretty sure you smacking in the head won't do anything, he thought. *Touché self, touché.*

It did however give him enough time to distance himself from the monster. Lexx scrambled towards the assembly area doors. He could hear LJ right behind him; he looked back in his peripheral and could have sworn he saw the thing down on all fours, like an animal. He bust through the double doors into the large open area where the construction vehicles were built. The beast came barreling through the doors but was greeted by Lexx, who had the shotgun ready and aimed. He let the last shell go, blasting the beast right square on! It was peppered with buckshot; the blast itself sent the creature back through the doors.

That should give me a second to try and find something, Lexx thought.

He looked all around. Over on a workbench lay a giant monkey wrench. He went over and grabbed it. It was at least two feet long. He opened the claw so that it was open a few inches.

Let's see how he likes taking one of these to the head.

Lexx began running for the other side of the room when the monster came bursting back through the doors, sending the doors flying off in different directions. He hid himself out of the beast's sight and waited for it to get close enough so he could bring the business end of the wrench down on its head.

LJ sat there for a moment, hunched over. It began to sniff the air. It was trying to smell Lexx out. Lexx smelt himself.

Oh man. I stink, he thought.

The monster began to slowly walk in the direction of where Lexx was hiding.

C'mon, get closer you bastard.

It crept closer and closer. Lexx waited. He had to time this just right. If he missed, well, he could be dead. He was determined to bring the open claw right down on the thing's skull. It may have shaken off the bullet, maybe Jeremy hit it wrong. There's no way it could survive a direct blow to the head with this bad boy.

Now!

Lexx screamed inside his head as he swung out and brought the wrench down on the beast's skull as hard as he could. The claw sunk into meaty flesh and hit bone. The wrench end pushed through, breaking through the thick plate of bone and ripping into its brain. There was a loud crack and the beast went tense, pulling Lexx forward. It lashed out in a last ditch effort and sent Lexx flying. He hit a fabrication machine and slunk to the floor. What was once LJ convulsed and then went limp. A thick and dark, coagulated blood gelled onto the floor from the wound.

Lexx watched as the beast died. His own eyes opened and shut, he felt himself drifting in and out of consciousness. He mind went to Tori. He knew Jeremy would get her out. He's a good guy. She'd be safe with him.

Man, she was a good kisser.

What he'd give for a kiss from her right now. To feel those soft lips one last time. To run his hands across her curves. If it wasn't the end of the world, he would have gone the full shebang and taken her to a nice dinner at the Red Lobster.

Oh, man. Cheese biscuits...

And with that, everything went black.

***

Jeremy put his head in his hands.

"God, I know we don't talk much. I don't even know

if I'm doing this right but you knew my mom, right? Well, she said she knew you. Look, I'm still not very happy with you, with what happened to my parents and then what happened to my mom. But, if you could just help me out here. I know it would mean lot to her. Uh, thanks. I mean, amen."

He lifted his head and for a moment pictured there being a vision of what he should do scrolling across the wall. Except there was nothing. No vision. No sign. Nothing. Thanks God.

Tori was out of her catatonic state and was looking around the room. Maybe she'd be easier to move now. Out of everyone in the group, she was the one he least expected to shut down like that. She had been so assertive before. Almost to a fault. She could have easily been the leader of the group. Except no, that all had to fall on Jeremy. The nineteen year old was the only adult in the group. Typical.

"Radio," Tori said.

Great, now she's saying random words, he thought.

"A radio," she said again a little louder.

"That's great Tori, maybe we can find a radio station that's playing a great song to die to!"

Jeremy begins to hum the tune of a song about it being "the end of the world as we know it". He finds this amusing. Tori does not.

"No, fuck-tard. A CB radio!"

Jeremy looked at her. She had snapped out of it.

"You're back!" he said as he went over and threw his arms around her.

"Yeah, I'm back. Sorry about that. Now let go!"

She pushed him aside and scrambled over to the CB radio that was sitting on the bottom shelf of a lone bookshelf. She turned it on and started fiddling with the knobs and switches.

"It still has power! My dad was friends with a lot of

truckers when I was younger. I think I remember the main chatter channel. Give me a sec," she said.

"I am so glad you are back," said a relived Jeremy. She ignored him and sat the radio down on the table. She held up the handheld microphone.

"Here goes nothing," she said, taking a deep breath. Jeremy crossed his fingers. She clicked the microphone's button on.

"Hello? Hello? If there's anyone nearby, we're off of I-95 between Highway 80 and the airport exit. We are in need of assistance. Hello? Anybody read me?"

She let go of the button and they waited for a response. One minute passed. Another minute. She tried again and got nothing but silence. Jeremy started to realize that they would most likely not leave this building. They were going to die here. He was about to suggest that they make a try for the truck when the radio clicked on.

"Hello?" a voice said.

Chapter Thirty

"Hello! Hello! Who is this?" Tori screamed into the microphone.

There was some static for a moment.

"My name is Josh. I'm a truck driver and I'm going to be passing you shortly. What's your twenty? Over."

"We're trapped in the construction building. It's me, another man, and maybe one more. Our truck is surrounded and we can't get out. Over."

There was silence.

"He thinking it over," Tori said. "He's just thinking it over."

Jeremy wasn't sure if she was trying to convince him or herself.

Maybe both, he thought.

The radio clicked back on.

"Can you get out of the building and to the interstate?"

She looked at Jeremy. He shook his head. With the mass group of zombies out front, that would be a near impossible task. Possibly even suicidal.

"I don't think so Tori," he said.

She held the mic back up to her mouth and paused before turning it back on.

"That's gonna be really hard for us. We're surrounded. Over."

"Sounds like you don't have many options then," Josh said. "I'll be there in ten minutes. If you can make it to the interstate, I can pick you up. Over."

Jeremy's mind began to problem solve. If they could just elude the zombies, they might be able to make it to 95. They still had the rifle and almost a full clip in the last pistol. It's not impossible. Technically.

"Let's do it," he said. She nodded.

"Josh? That is affirmative for pick up. Over."

"Good. Ten minutes. Be there. Over and out."

Tori sat the mic down on the table.

"Alright, what's the plan?" she asked. She saw the wheels turning in Jeremy's head. And she was right, he did have a plan.

"Ok, plan's this: We make a run for the front door and make our away across the field to the interstate. We have enough ammo to only shoot when necessary. We need to conserve it the best as possible. But that's it. We run like hell."

"That's a great plan," she said. He didn't catch any of her trademark sarcasm in that. She really meant it. It was simple and it was efficient. They could get out of here. They were going to get out of here.

Jeremy took a deep breath and then opened the door. He peered out into the hallway. Nothing was out there. No zombies. No monster. He motioned for Tori to follow him. She did and they made their way towards the front of the building. So far so good.

When they entered back into the foyer, there was no sign of Lexx or the monster. There were, however, several zombies in the room. Jeremy glanced back at Tori.

"Only shoot if you have to," he whispered.

She nodded and they began to snake through the living dead. The first two were slow and did not even realize they had been passed. The third one did notice however. It reached out, but missed grabbing Tori by the arm. The rest of the group became increasingly aware of the two humans moving through their midst. They began to moan.

Jeremy wondered if they had the ability to communicate, because the moans drew in more dead from the surrounding hallways. Or maybe they were just attracted to the noise, like the alarm from yesterday. Either way, more were coming in their direction.

"C'mon! Almost to the door!" He yelled, giving up on being quiet. It was pointless at that point. The dead knew they were there. They broke out into a sprint towards the door. One zombie got too close for comfort, so Jeremy fired a round point-blank into the thing's skull. Grayish brain matter covered one of its buddies but it did not seem to mind too much. It just kept on coming.

Tori passed Jeremy while he was dispatching the zombie and was holding the door open, waiting for him to reach her. He ran through the door and she slammed it shut behind them.

"Thanks," he said, turning in her direction.

"Look out!" She yelled.

She pushed him aside and rammed the barrel of the rifle into a z's throat who was about to grab Jeremy. She pulled the trigger and the bullet traveled out the back of the zombie's head, through the shoulder of another, and finally grazed across the back of one's neck, severing the spinal cord. It fell to its knees and then over. The one who took it in the shoulder stumbled backwards, never got its footing back, and tripped over his fallen comrade.

"Nice shot!" Jeremy yelled. He gave her the thumbs up. She smiled and pointed towards the interstate. A white Ford F-350 with a stake body bed was pulling up and they were still a good fifty yards away.

Please don't leave us, please don't leave us, Jeremy began to chant in his head, as he ran as fast as he could in the direction of the truck.

***

Lexx opened his eyes. He looked around and was confused on where he was.

What happened? He thought as he sat up straight.

He then noticed the dead monster with a wrench

stuck in its head. Blood had stopped from oozing, but a thick puddle of goo covered the floor.

Oh, yeah...

There was a crash off to his left. His head rolled to the left. A small group of zombies were knocking tools off a workbench. Lexx stood up and reached for the wrench. It was stuck.

"Wow, I really got that in there," he muttered.

He gave it another tug. Nothing. Taking a deep breath first, he then yanked on the giant wrench and it pulled free with a sickening slosh. The zombies took notice of the commotion.

"Uh-oh. Hey guys..."

Lexx turned and ran for the door. Maybe Jeremy and Tori had not left yet. Maybe they were waiting in the truck. He hoped so, as he ran for the back loading dock. Turning to head in that direction, he stopped suddenly when he heard a rifle fire from the front of the building.

Tori!

He about-faced for the front of the building. There were several zombies still in the main room, but there was a trail of extra-dead ones leading towards the door.

Jeremy and Tori must have come through this way.

He brought the wrench down on the head of a dead elderly woman. She crumpled like a rag doll. He had to take out the rest of them because they had swarmed around the front door. Several zombies later and he was good to go.

But when the path was finally cleared and he looked through the glass front door, he could see Jeremy and Tori running towards the interstate. They were booking it. He ran outside.

"Hey guys! Tori!" He yelled, waving his hands in the air. Zombies were taking notice of him and beginning to moan and shuffle towards him, but he didn't care.

"Guys!"

They couldn't hear him. He yelled as he ran, swinging the wrench wildly. Zombies left and right fell, as Lexx plowed his way through the crowd. Like a machine, he moved steadily through the mob of the dead. He watched as a truck pulled up and they both climbed in.

"No!" He yelled.

The truck drove away.

He watched as the truck took off down the interstate.

This could't be happening. This cannot be happening.

The dead were closing in all around him. He stopped, breathing heavily. His mind began to tail spin. He looked at the interstate, then back at the building, and then finally to all the zombies that were quickly crowding around him.

"Fuck."

Chapter Thirty One

"I saw him! I swear I saw him!"

Tori was yelling hysterically that she saw Lexx outside of the building as they drove away.

"He was trying to flag us down! He's alive! He's alive! We have to go back," she screamed.

"No way."

The truck driver never took his eyes off the road. He was young, maybe mid-twenties. He wore one of those reflective yellow vests that construction workers wear. His clothes were dirty and tattered. It looked like he had been in a few skirmishes with the dead himself. His calmly-spoken words caused the truck to fall painfully silent. It did not take long for Tori to break that silence.

"What do you mean, 'no way'?" she asked.

"I mean, no way. It's not safe. Too many zombies," he responded, just as calm as before.

Jeremy watched as the man's hand tightened on the steering wheel. He must have been anticipating what was about to happen next.

Tori flipped her lid.

"You bastard! Turn this truck around right now or let us out! That's our friend back there! We can't just leave him behind! Stop this truck!"

"Yeah, I'm gonna go with a 'no' on that one," he said, breaking eye contact with the road and looking Tori dead in the eye. Jeremy was sure this only infuriated her more. She reached for the pistol that Jeremy set on the dashboard.

"Tori, no!" He yelled.

But it was too late.

She had the gun pressed against the driver's head.

"You are going to turn this truck around. And we will get our friend," she said, each word as firm and calm as he had spoken earlier.

It was almost scary how calm she was.

"You know what lady? On second thought, I really want to turn this truck around and go get your friend. Yeah, let's do that," the driver said.

He spun the truck around in the middle of the highway, crossing over the grassy median and began to travel back towards the building. Tori put the gun down on her lap. The driver would eye it cautiously every few seconds. Jeremy felt kind of bad for her behavior. The guy did pick them up and all. He wanted to find Lexx too though.

Best to just let the woman handle it, he thought.

The truck came back up to the spot where he picked them up from. Most of the zombies that were on the highway were now roaming the area in front of the building. There was still a large number of them and no sign of Lexx. There must have been at least a couple hundred zombies out there. The front doors to the building were closed and a group of dead were banging on the glass. He must have retreated back inside and secured the doors somehow.

"Alright lady, you got a plan?" he asked.

"Yeah, let's go get him."

"That's what I thought," he said, shaking his head.

"Look over there. You see all those zombies? We don't have the weapons to take on all of them. You probably don't have any ammo, do you? The pistol you just held to my head probably doesn't even have any bullets in it does it?"

"Three."

"Okay, well that may have blown my head clean off but it ain't gonna help you get to that building and your lover boy."

She began to respond to that but he held his finger to his mouth and shushed her.

"Luckily for you, I have a plan. I always have a plan."

With that he opened his door, stepped out and reached into the toolbox hanging from under the bed of the truck. He pulled out what looked like a large megaphone. There was a round, flat magnet on the bottom and he took it and stuck it to the roof of the cab. A lone wire hung down from the device and he cracked open the window to pull the wire through.

"I wired up this little puppy to drive the guys in the field nuts. They love it when I come to the jobsites blaring music. I like to let 'em know I'm coming."

He unplugs a mp3 player from the audio jack in the stereo and plugs it into the megaphone wire. He hums to himself as he scrolls through his play lists.

"Oh yeah, this is it. Okay, listen up."

He looked up at Jeremy and Tori.

"We are going to drive over there. And by we, I mean mostly me. I will be blasting some sweet tunes through this here megaphone. Once we get close enough, the nice gun-lady here will jump out, and retrieve the aforementioned lover boy. You, my friend," he motioned at Jeremy. "You will get into the back of the truck. Don't worry, the gates may rattle, but they ain't poppin' out. You are gonna be the catcher."

"The catcher?" Jeremy asked.

"Yes. The catcher. That is what I said. You see, while you and I are going to be causing a very, noisy distraction, your lady friend here is going to be getting your other buddy and booking it to the second floor."

"Why the second floor?" Tori asked.

"Because you are going to jump into the back of the truck when we drive by and then we are gonna vámanos on out of here."

Both Tori and Jeremy just stared at the man.

Was he serious? Did he really expect them to just jump from the second floor onto a moving truck?

This had to be the craziest thing that Jeremy had ever heard.

"So, you ready?" the driver asked.

"Man, are you serious? We can't do that!" Jeremy yelled.

"Well, like I said before, it doesn't look like you have many options here. Look, I know it sounds a little crazy but-"

"A little crazy?" Tori chimed in.

"Ok, it's crazy. But it's gonna work. I swears."

Jeremy thought it over. The guy was right. They did not have many options and time was running short. If they were going to do something, they had to do it quick. He shook his head and looked at Tori. He could see that she was starting to come around to it as well. What other choice did they have?

"Hey man," Jeremy started. "What's your name again?"

"Josh."

"What did you do before all this, Josh?" Tori asked.

"I worked for a local plumbing and mechanical company. I delivered material to the jobsites."

Jeremy and Tori looked at each other.

"So, you're a plumber?"

"No. I drive trucks basically."

This was fantastic, Jeremy thought.

"Ok, let's do this," Josh said as he pushed play on his mp3 player. A familiar bass line blared through the megaphone. Jeremy couldn't remember the name of the song until the first line came through the speaker.

"I CAN'T STAND IT, I KNOW YOU PLANNED IT..."

"Beastie Boys? Really?" Tori asked.

"Heck yeah! I love this song!" Jeremy said.

Josh pointed his finger at Jeremy.

"I knew I liked you man. Now let's go get your friend."

**

Lexx could not believe they left him. He could, but he couldn't. They didn't even look for him. They just left. And drove off into the mother-fucking sunset.

Well, you did tell him to get her out of here, he thought to himself. *Yeah, but they could have at least looked for me.*

He took his frustration out on the zombies that wandered in from the hallways. When he came back inside he used his wrench to hold the doors together, so the dead were just piling up in front of the doors. They beat on the glass, but that was some damn solid glass. It would hold up.

The zombies that wandered in from the hallways on the other hand, they got the blunt end of Lexx's anger. He found a large trophy that the company had won for "Most Innovative" and was using it to bash in the brains of the undead. One by one they would come in and one by one they would get their heads caved in.

What am I going to do? I can't just keep doing this for the rest of my life. I gotta go do some-

He stopped. Music. He heard music. It was coming from outside. He smashed the nearest zombie in the head and turned back to the windows. He found a spot where he could see past the dead and his mouth dropped open.

The truck that had picked up Tori and Jeremy was headed straight for the building. The massive white truck was barreling straight towards him, sending zombies flying with the brush guard and running others over. A speaker on top of the truck was blaring Beastie Boys' "Sabotage." As the truck got closer it turned, putting the passenger side parallel with the building. Tori was hanging out of the window, waving with a big smile on her face.

"Coming to get you!" she yelled. "Be right back!"

The truck pulled away and led the zombies away from the building. Lexx's heart leapt. He couldn't believe it. They came back for him. He knew he was having a hard time believing they left him, but this was a lot harder to believe. They came back for him. The truck circled for a minute and then started to come back towards the building. It came right up to the door and Tori jumped out and ran to the building.

Lexx immediately went to the door and removed the wrench. She leapt into his arms and they held each other briefly before she pushed herself off.

"We have to hurry! We have to get to the second floor!" she yelled, grabbing him by the wrist and directing him towards the giant spiral staircase.

"The second floor?" Lexx asked.

"No time to explain! Come on!"

They ran for the stairs and began the climb. Zombies were now pouring in from both the hallways and the outside. They shambled towards the stairs and began the struggle of getting up the steps. Most of them would lose their footing and fall, but a few were slowly making it. But by then, Tori and Lexx had already made it to the top and were running towards the walkway that led to the balcony on the window-side of the room. There were small patio chairs and tables set up there. A few single-serve coffee makers sat in the corner. It must have been a place where admins would come and enjoy a nice cup of joe while on break.

Screams. Runners were in the building.

"Lexx, you gotta break the glass so we can jump onto the back of the truck!" Tori yelled frantically.

He shook his head.

"Tori..."

The runners reached the foyer. There were five of

them and they ran for the stairs, shrieking madly as they went.

"Hurry Lexx!"

"Tori, that glass isn't gonna break. I watched them beat on it the whole time you were gone. It's not gonna break..."

Her face fell.

"But we have to. It's the only way out."

He set his wrench down against the glass and pulled her in close to him. He took a deep breath, breathing in her scent for what could be one last time. Her heart raced against his chest.

"I'm sorry. It's just not going to happen."

She looked up at him and then laid her head on his chest. He felt so helpless. The runners were at the top of the stairs. It would be seconds before they were on them. He would do his best to fight them off but he knew that against five of them, he didn't stand a chance. They had never taken the runners on in a fight. He was so angry with himself. So angry that he let her come back for him.

And that's when he felt it.

The anger pulsed through his veins. It seethed through his skin. The rage. The rage that Jeremy had spoken about experiencing after his mother was killed. The rage that caused the Lumberjack to blindly slaughter everyone around him. Lexx was feeling the rage. And he was fucking pissed.

He grabbed the wrench right as the first runner reached them. He reared back and swung, taking the zombie's head clear off its shoulders. The other runners paused at this, and for the first time showed hesitation. This brought a smile to his face and gave Lexx enough time to turn and throw the wrench as hard as he could through the window.

The glass shattered into a million pieces.

He heard the truck honk its horn. It was there parked below the window; Jeremy waiting in the back, waving for them to jump. Lexx looked at Tori and grabbed her hand before leaping out of the window. They hit the truck bed with a thud and rolled.

"We got 'em! Go! Go!" Jeremy yelled, banging on the roof of the truck's cab.

The truck driver gave the thumbs up and floored it. As they sped off, Lexx watched as the runners tried to follow and wound up jumping through the window only to splatter themselves against the ground. He felt himself relax and the rage slowly dissipated, as they drove off and away from that nightmare.

Epilogue

Jeremy watched the scenery pass by outside the window. They were well into the country now. Maybe thirty minutes from Statesboro. Nothing but trees and empty cotton fields out here. Peaceful.

Once they got out of Savannah, they explained to Josh everything that had happened with Ben and how the whole plan was to go to his parents' house. Now with Ben gone, they weren't really sure where they would go. They assumed to continue to go out west somewhere; they just weren't sure where.

Josh laughed at this. He explained that he too was heading west and that he was hoping to find his wife and her family. They left him a note saying they were alive and went to their family's hunting club. There was a cabin up there and plenty of room for Josh's family and Jeremy's group to share. They gladly accepted his invitation.

"It's funny how the Lord works out things like that," Josh said.

"The Lord?" Jeremy asked.

"Yeah, Jesus. You ever heard of him?"

Jeremy stared at Josh in disbelief.

Another Christian?

"What are the odds," he muttered to himself, but it was louder than he expected.

"Odds?" Josh asked.

"Oh, sorry. It's just weird. You're the third Christian I've met since this started. Well, I knew my mom before, but she's played a part in this too. I lost her in the beginning."

"I'm sorry to hear that man. I lost my niece."

Jeremy nodded.

Everyone's lost someone, he thought.

It was a part of life now it seemed. You were going

to lose people. Mom, the Padre and Ben. All gone. Mom was hard, but it surprised Jeremy how much he missed Padre and Ben. The time he spent with Ben was brief and with Padre even briefer, but the two men had greatly impacted his life.

Josh was smiling.

"What's so funny man?" Jeremy asked.

"Oh nothing's funny," he said. "It's just the fact that you met another Christian. Blows my mind. Makes it pretty clear He's got a hand in all this."

"I'm not really in the mood for a Bible lesson right now, but what do you mean?"

"What do I mean? Think about it man. What are the odds that I would be driving by that building exactly when y'all had no way out? That you two would find that CB radio in that office? You know I would have driven by yesterday, but for some unknown reason I felt like I should stay at my brother-in-law's house last night. So I did. Almost died because of it."

"Yeah..."

"And what are the odds that you met another Christian? First, you got your mother your whole life trying to get you into church and whatnot. Then you got the Padre guy you were telling me about, and how he was telling you that God wasn't responsible for this evil going on, and that maybe He was the one looking out for you. And now me. In the past three days, when the world has gone to hell, you just so happen to meet three believers? What are those odds Jeremy? Have you ever thought about playing the lottery?"

Jeremy nodded and went back to looking out the window. It was strange, he would give him that. Coincidence, maybe. But providence? No, he was not ready to think about that yet. He remembered his prayer from the custodian's office. Maybe God really did hear him. Maybe his prayer was answered. Could the Padre have been right? Did God have a plan for all of this? Was he going to use this plague to somehow do something great?

Jeremy was unsure. He didn't know but he was sure this Josh-guy was going to tell him. The guy seemed alright so far. Weird sense of humor, but okay as far as Jeremy was concerned. He peeked back to the bed of the truck.

Lexx and Tori were sitting with their backs to the cab. The two had been inseparable since they rescued Lexx. He couldn't blame them. Jeremy was really happy for the two of them. While at first Tori may have been attractive to him and maybe he did have a little bit of a crush on the woman at first, over the past few days, she had grown more into a big sister figure. And he liked it that way. And Lexx, well, Lexx was Lexx. He was glad to have him back. Jeremy smiled and for the first time in a while knew things were going to be okay. He, unlike much of the world around him, was alive.

END OF BOOK ONE

Acknowledgements

Thanks go out to:
The real Avery, for reading the first draft and bugging me to finish it.
Chad D, in the real apocalypse, I'm coming to your house.
Danielle M, for your reader's insight.
My Mother, for giving me your love of reading and weird things.
Jeremy and Meredith G, for helping Laura and I slay the zombies in our lives.
CJ and Hailey H, the best nephew and niece ever.
George Romero, Robert Kirkman, and Max Brooks for helping shape zombie lore.
Muse, wore out Absolution when I wrote this.
Stubbs, when Hollywood comes a knockin', we'll finally make that zombie movie.
Xavier Martinez, for making the coolest book cover ever.
Christina S, for your help editing and proofreading.
And last, but not least, to all of my teachers over the years. Sorry I gave you such a hard time.
And everybody else, thanks for sticking with me!

Also:
Jeep is a Registered Trademark of General Motors
Coke is a Registered Trademark Of Coca Cola Co.
"Sabotage" and its lyrics are owned by Beastie Boys.
Wal-Mart is a Registered Trademark of Wal-Mart

About the Author

When he's not writing about himself in third-person, Josh Vasquez lives in Savannah, GA with his wife Laura. It is currently zombie-free.

He says, "You're welcome."

Feel free to email him what you liked, disliked, or any questions about the story at beencalled@gmail.com He checks this email weekly, but will make the best effort to get back to you. If you want, he will add you to his contact list and send you updates about his work. He promises not to spam you or fill your inbox with cat pictures.

You can also follow the author on Twitter
@beencalled

And check out updates on the world of A New Death at:
savannahzombienovel.com

Before You Go

If you are reading this, then you my friend, are holding a book.

Made of paper. And ink.

You are super dedicated. (Or you don't like reading on a screen, which is cool too.)

You bought a paperback version of this book, which means you went above and beyond to read my work. This shows character.

You should make everyone aware of how awesome you are and go leave a review on Amazon.

Seriously, go do it. (Right now.)

People will thank you publically in the streets and children will sing your praises. (They might not, but I sure as heck will!)

Thank you so much for your support,
Josh Vasquez

Also Available

A New Death: CJ's Story (Kindle)
In this short story, meet thirteen year old CJ, the nephew of Josh from A New Death. Find out how his family gets out of Savannah and out to their cabin in the country when the dead start coming back to life.

A New Darkness
The continuing story of Jeremy and company. Will Jeremy survive the zombie apocalypse? Will Josh find his family alive? Will Lexx ever find more Coke? Find out in the thrilling sequel to *A New Death*!

Made in the USA
Charleston, SC
11 October 2014